One thing about covens that you need to know if you do not know it already: no guys.

This is not a sexist thing. It's that guys don't have the same level of psychic development as girls and women. I mean, sure, there are guy witches. And you get the occasional wizard. But did you ever see a wizard in a circle of thirteen? Not if those witches know what they're doing.

And I think guys are distracting to somebody who needs to develop all her powers. The thing to do if you are a witch is to develop those powers then use them to get the guys you want. Not that that is a problem in Jurupa. The guys at Richard Milhous Nixon Union High School are to die *from*.

So the first advice on being a witch is find twelve more girls who want to be one. The second advice is no guys, no matter how cute they are. *Especially* if they are cute.

DOUGLAS REES

MAJIX

Notes From a Serious teen Witch

HARLEQUIN®
TEEN

HARLEQUIN®
TEEN

ISBN-13: 978-0-373-21017-6

MAJIX: NOTES FROM A SERIOUS TEEN WITCH

Copyright © 2010 by Douglas Rees

Recycling programs
for this product may
not exist in your area.

This edition published by arrangement with Harlequin Books S.A.

For questions and comments about the quality of this book
please contact us at Customer_eCare@Harlequin.ca.

www.HarlequinTEEN.com

Printed in U.S.A.

To Lisi

A WITCH NEVER COMPLAINS

MY NAME IS KESTREL. Kestrel Murphy. Never call me Susan. Whoever heard of a witch named Susan?

Which is what I am. Witch is what I am. I do magick, which is what a witch does. A year ago I was on the white side. Lately, I've been leaning toward the black.

I blame the universe. What's the point in being a nice little white witch in the kind of universe I've got? Jennifer used to say, "You choose your own universe." Which is bogus. Because I would never have chosen a universe like this one. If I could choose my own universe, I would choose to be a white witch in it. But this is someone else's universe, and it sucks.

Black makes a lot of sense in a universe like this.

Not that I'm complaining. A WITCH NEVER COM-PLAINS. But if I did, I'd have a lot to complain about.

For instance: Jurupa.

For instance: Why I am stuck in Jurupa.

For instance: Jennifer.

For instance: The Rentz.

For instance: Richard Milhous Nixon Union High School.
They are not in order. There is no order. Not in this universe.

Jurupa is where I am living. If you call it living. The J is an
H. The Us are OOs. Hooroopah. It's an ancient Indian word
meaning barf. I mean, that's what it sounds like. Ancient Indian
barf.

Jurupa is in Southern California, where it is too hot to live
if you are not a cactus, and you have to chew the air to get the
oxygen out of it. It is maybe an hour and a half from Hollywood and maybe an hour from Palm Springs, and it is on the
other side of the moon from both. If you can't make it in a
place like Hollywood or Palm Springs or Silicon Valley, and you
want to stay in California, Jurupa is the kind of place you end
up. It's the smog and the heat. They attract dumb people. You
know—regular folks. Normals. The kind of people who are
products of seventeen generations of inbreeding, which shows
up every time they try to think, or talk, or cross the street
without help.

I did not ask to come here. I am from Northern California,
where the people are smart and the weather changes. But the
no-good, rotten, clueless, totally bogus universe has dumped
me here and abandoned me. I will find a way to get even with
it.

Which will require studying gramarye. Which is the other
name for witchcraft. And which looks a lot like grammar.
Which is not an accident.

Jennifer told me, before the universe took her away and sent
her to Kansas City, that back in the Middle Ages people
thought reading was a magick thing, like witchcraft. So when
it was time to burn the witches, they burned the people who
could read along with them, probably to save wood. People
were really stupid, then. Like they are in Jurupa, now.

I am in real danger. Either I will be burned alive or bored
to death.

I Must Get Out of Here.

But sending me to Jurupa was not the worst thing the universe has done to me. It is second worst. The worst was why it sent me. Because of BD.

BD is Big Daddy. The male half of The Rentz. My spawner. The male co-babymaker of me with Mommy Angel, the rest of The Rentz. BD is this major computer jock. He's got his own company and he's a sort of growth attached to it. He likes to sit in a dark room with five or six computer screens going at once, and smoke and eat ice cream. If they came up with ice cream he could smoke, he'd have it made.

He did have it made. Until he had his heart attack. Which was a big one. And now he can't have any more ice cream or tobacco or stress. Stress means his company, which he sold for major bucks. And me, who he couldn't sell. So here I am, whooping it up in Jurupa. Mommy Angel says it's just until BD's heart is stronger (meaning: "Until he can stand having you around again"). But I think it's permanent. He can't handle me developing my powers. Or smoking. BD and I do not compute. Neither do I and Mommy Angel.

Plus, the way they sent me here was like getting rid of a dog you don't want. And Jurupa is the pound.

I was sitting around in my room minding my own business worrying about BD and wondering how much longer until he came home from the hospital, which we knew by then would be soon.

Mommy Angel knocks on the door and says, "Susan, may I talk to you?"

This is weird because she has never asked before in my whole life if she can talk to me. If she wants to, she does. If she doesn't, she doesn't. If I want to talk to her and she wants to talk to me, she does. If she doesn't, she gets a catalog and starts looking at stuff.

So I open the door because I am curious. And also because I am scared.

And I was right to be scared. Because what Mommy Angel says in her niciest way is as scary as a demon that's gotten loose from its pentagram and hasn't had lunch yet.

"Susan, dear, your father and I have been talking. Actually, I've also been talking with his doctor. And with your aunt."

I know I have an aunt, but I have never met her. She is BD's sister.

"You know, we're having kind of an emergency around here," Mommy Angel says, and she sighs.

"Yeah," I say. "I know."

"Well, your father's doctor says that your daddy is going to need a long quiet time to get really, really well. And he knows how your daddy had his heart attack. And we've told him about some of the other things you've—well, some of the other things that have happened around here recently. And he thinks it might be a good idea if you went someplace else for a while while your daddy gets all better." And she puts her hand on top of mine.

"Well, there just aren't that many places to send a good little girl who isn't in trouble or doing drugs or anything," she says. "And I thought of Ted's sister. Why don't I ask her if she can take you in for a little while? And do you know what she said? She said, 'Of course. Send her as soon as you like.'"

I'm leaving. I'm leaving because my daddy doesn't want me. That's what she's telling me. That's what she's saying.

"But Daddy hates his sister," I say. "You can't send me there."

"He doesn't hate her," Mommy Angel smiles. "They just don't get along."

"I don't want to go anyplace," I say. "I live here. This is my home."

"Of course it is, honey," Mommy Angel says. "And I don't want you to go. Daddy doesn't want you to go. But this is an emergency. And we all have to do something extra because of it. Now, you don't have to stay down there forever. It'll just be for a few months at the most. Probably just a semester. Or maybe two. But you're still our baby, and of course we'll take you back the very day we can."

"Why not send Daddy away? Some place nice and quiet?"

"He'll do better at home," Mommy Angel says. "And he'll do better with me to take care of him."

"I'll help you," I say. "I can do healing spells and change bandages and stuff."

"Your daddy doesn't need bandages," Mommy Angel says with a bogus laugh. "He needs quiet and rest."

I can be quiet. I even offer to stay off the roof. But no deal. The fix is in. I'm out of there. And now I am here. In Jurupa. With Aunt Ariel, the Witch Sneak.

Aunt Ariel is BD's big sister. I mean, big. She is not one of the thin people. She is also a witch, the wussie white kind. The kind who says, "Blesséd be," about everything. Lame.

Not that she doesn't have something. I mean, I had to get my psychic powers from somewhere. Probably we have some ancient crones flying around our family tree and we get our powers from them. And even wimpola white magick can work. But you shouldn't use it in a bogus, sneaky way on your own family. Which she did.

I mean, I'd been smoking for a year. Ever since Jennifer went to Kansas City. BD told me to stop, even though I only smoked his brand. Mommy Angel told me to stop. Like I cared. They were my cigarettes, and my lungs.

Aunt Ariel got me to stop the first day I was here. And she did it in a totally rotten white magick way.

When she caught me with my pack of cancer sticks, she didn't lecture me or tell me all the stuff that I already know, like it kills you. She just had one of her coven come over. Danae, who's about the size of a double-sided refrigerator and lifts weights.

She had Danae stand in the middle of the patio. Then she had me try to lift Danae's arm from her side while Danae tried not to let me do it. No way could I move that arm. Then Danae took my arm and tried to do the same thing. I'm not built like Danae, but I'm strong. Thin and tough, like wire. And I cast a spell for strength. No way could Danae move my arm, though I had to work hard to hold it tight.

Then Ariel said, "All right, Kestrel dear, light up."

So I did.

I took three puffs, and my aunt raised my arm over my head like it didn't weigh anything. My strength wasn't there. Then she held hands with me while she held hands with Danae. We all stood here like beads on a string. Aunt Ariel told me to take three more puffs. Then she told me to go over to Danae and try to move her arm. I did the same thing, lifted it like Danae had never bench-pressed three hundred pounds in her life. Where did her strength go?

I looked at the weed in my hand.

My aunt said, "Now, Kestrel, just imagine what that's doing to your aura."

I ground the thing out and went into the house. Haven't touched one since.

It's been a week. My naughty little body keeps saying, "Hey, Kestrel, isn't it time to light up?"

And my good witch brain keeps saying, "Shut up, stupid."

Because I need to keep my aura in shape. Because I will need all my powers to get through this bogus, no-win rotten life I'm in.

So today, right now, in my room in Jurupa with the door closed and a chair pushed against it, I am starting this grimoire. I will fill it with magick and develop my powers until they are strong enough to make the universe do what I want it to do, which is: Make BD well enough so I can go home. Get me out of here. Get Jennifer back to California.

Because if there is one thing I know about the universe, it's that it is not blesséd. The universe is a bad place and you have to learn how to control it. That's what real magick is all about.

THE CRAFT

THIS CHAPTER IS ADVICE about becoming a witch. But it is also more about me. Because in case you are reading this a hundred years from now, it will mean that I became a very powerful and mighty witch and you will want to know all about how I did it.

So this chapter will give you advice on how to get started. Also, it will prove that I AM NOT COMPLAINING. I AM ONLY EXPLAINING WHY I WENT TO THE BLACK.

For instance: High school.

Especially: This high school. Richard Milhous Nixon Union High. Which is where Aunt Ariel makes me go. Which sucks.

The first day of ninth grade, I showed up in solid black. Black T-shirt, black jeans, black shoes, black glasses. I had my seventeen earrings on, and three new green streaks in my hair. I mean, I looked like me.

But every other kid was wearing a white polo shirt and tan slacks. It's the uniform. An antigang thing. No problem. I do not join gangs. But I looked like a crow in a flock of pigeons.

It took about two minutes for some teacher to haul me into the principal's office. His name's Dr. Gorringe. Which should be pronounced Garbage, and is, when he can't hear it.

HERE IS WHAT HAPPENED

Garbage Gorringe has a little gray hair, cut short and combed up stiff in front. His head is bald and grows up behind this hair fence like some perverted basketball. He's playing with a pencil, tapping it on the desk.

GG: You are out of uniform.

ME: This is my uniform.

GG: You are a student here and you will dress like everyone else.

ME: I am a witch, and I will dress like what I am.

GG: If you have financial hardship, uniforms will be provided for you out of school funds.

ME: Nobody has enough financial hardship to dress like that.

GG: This school has a zero-tolerance policy.

ME: You're a zero, and it tolerates you.

GG: If you are not willing to conform, you will be suspended.

ME: Cool!

THE END

So I was sent home on the first day. Hey, I was practically sent home the first minute. I felt so good. I'd figured how to get out of ninth grade without even faking sick. Which I could have done. I have a spell that could have had me Juruping long enough to convince Garbage I was dying. I just invoke Moloch, the demon of gluttony. Then, when no one's looking, I stick my finger down my throat. Works every time.

I figured I'd spend the rest of my time in Jurupa staying home and developing my powers. But Aunt Ariel said no.

Anyway, she calls all twelve of the women in her coven, and they all go down to Gorringe's office after school that day. They are all dressed like me, in black, black, and black. Even though they are old cows in their thirties and forties.

Aunt Ariel drags me along. She tells Gorringe that it's my religious right to dress like that and if he doesn't lift the suspension, not only will her church, the Temple of Ishtar, sue the school district, she will sue him personally.

And one of the other witches leans forward and puts her card on Gorringe's desk.

ANNE ROTHENBERG, JD
Attorney-at-Law
2367 Ramona Avenue
Jurupa, CA 92506
555-7123
e-mail: suethebastards@quickpost.com

Which is why I'm back at Richard Milhous Nixon Union High School the next day, along with 1,622 other kids, each one of whom is another reason to hate it here. But I am wearing black, which is something.

And Gorringe hates me, which is also something. I see him look at me in the hall and then look past me, like the wall is really interesting.

I'd have some respect for my aunt if she'd at least used witchcraft. I mean, she's supposed to be this big-deal witch. But all she did was act like a parent or something.

But to be absolutely fair and because A WITCH NEVER LIES, I have to tell you that there is one good thing about Jurupa. Aunt Ariel's garage door. Which is solid black. Except for a white dot so small you can hardly see it. And on the other side of the door, it is solid white except for a black dot so small you can hardly see it. This is crazy, but at least it is crazy on purpose. The rest of the craziness in Jurupa is not. It is just people being crazy thinking that they are being sensible. Like Garbage Gorringe.

The garage is where Aunt Ariel meets with her coven. There's a long table set against the back wall, and red candles, and a rock that's supposed to be from some ancient temple in Babylon, and a pentagram on the floor. Every Friday night she and her twelve friends go out there and light candles and sing Babylonian Christmas carols or whatever, while the candles get everything smoky and smelling like mints. Then they wish blesséd be on everything, and break for white wine and cheese. It's really lame witchcraft.

But it's the only coven in town. At least as far as I know. At least I'll bet it is. And even if I wanted to I couldn't join because of the Rule of Thirteen. Which is: thirteen witches to a coven. And she's got thirteen.

There is another thing about covens that you need to know if you do not know it already: No guys.

This is not a sexist thing. It's that guys don't have the same level of psychic development as girls and women. I mean, sure, there are guy witches. And you get the occasional wizard. But did you ever see a wizard in a Circle of Thirteen? Not if those witches know what they're doing. It's like a battery with a weak cell.

And I think guys are distracting to somebody who needs to develop all her powers. The thing to do, if you are a witch, is to develop those powers, then use them to get the guys you want. Not that that is a problem in Jurupa. The guys at Richard Milhous Nixon Union High School are to die from. If they had a Stupid Contest, they would need a whole truckload of first prizes.

So the first advice on being a witch is: Find twelve more

girls who want to be one. The second advice is: No guys, no matter how cute they are. Especially if they are cute. But it doesn't matter because the rule is still: No guys.

And that brings me to the next advice on being a witch.

If you are going to be a witch and develop your powers, you need to spend a lot of time alone. The best place to be alone is up on the roof.

Even before I became a witch, I liked to climb up on top of the house. But because the top of the house is the best place in the world to be, I was not supposed to be up there. Because it's dangerous. But it was not dangerous to me because I move like a cat. I would climb up the trellis where the bougainvillea grew and just like a little kitten scamper up to the peak. I got scratches and earwigs from the bougainvillea, but that was okay. I was up on the roof.

I almost never did my roof thing when BD was home, only when Mommy Angel was. Because BD would get really T. Rex about it, but Mommy Angel just kind of wished I wouldn't.

HERE IS THE DIFFERENCE

BD: Susan, get the hell down off the roof NOW. I don't
       want you breaking the seal on it.

I come down.

The End

MA: Susan, darling, what are you doing up there?
ME: Nothing.
MA: Then come down and do it on the ground.
ME: I can't. It's *roof* nothing.
MA: I'm afraid you'll fall and hurt yourself.
ME: More people hurt themselves on the ground than
       on the roof.

MA: Susan, would you like to go shopping?
ME: After I'm done up here.

Mommy Angel sighs and goes away.
                                    The End

Up there on my roof, I could see the Ridges, which are low mountains that run along the east side of San Francisco Bay. They are gray in winter, green in spring, and golden the rest of the year. There are oak trees on them, which are green or blue, depending on how they are feeling. And on days when the clouds just touch the tops of the peaks and lie across the sky flat as a ceiling, you can see centaurs on the Ridges if you look. Never any other time.

From the other side of the roof you can see the Santa Cruz Mountains. They are real mountains, not just ridges. When the sun goes down behind them, they look like an old castle wall keeping you safe. When the fog comes in off the ocean, it builds up behind them and looks like a silent waterfall hanging in the sky. Then the sun goes down, and the waterfall flows in and covers up the stars. It is only regular clouds when it gets to my roof, but it is still way beautiful.

Plus, if you are smoking, and don't want The Rentz to know, the roof is a good place to do it.

And after I became a witch the roof was an even better place to be because it is closer to the moon, and the moon is very important to witches. That's what Jennifer said.

Jennifer was my friend. My best and only friend in seventh grade, which was where we met. And eighth grade. And she was the first witch I'd ever seen.

Jennifer always wore black and had long dangly earrings, three in one ear and four in the other. When she moved her head, she jingled, sort of. She never talked to anybody unless they talked to her first. Then what she usually said was, "No."

I never said anything to her. But I thought she was neat.

Because she always acted like she knew something you didn't. Something you would really want to know if you knew what it was you didn't know that she did. I would have liked to talk to her, but I couldn't think of anything to say that wouldn't make her say, "No."

Then we got teamed to do a country report, along with three other kids. Just in case it is a hundred years from now and you don't know what a country report is, I will explain. You get a country, which in this case was Brazil, and everybody has to do a part of the report. I got Way of Life. Jennifer got Government and Economy.

So we were sitting around in our study group trying to decide how to do the report, and Jennifer said, "I'm not doing Government and Economy. I'm doing Way of Life. Deal with it."

Kevin, who is our group's leader because he's the biggest suck-up of the five of us, says, "You can't do what you want. You have to do what the group decides."

"*You* have to do what the group decides," Jennifer says. "I'm doing Way of Life."

I don't care what part of the report I do. I don't want to do any of it. But here's a chance to talk to Jennifer. So after our meeting, which does not decide anything, I go up to her and I say, "Why do you want to do my stuff?"

"I don't," Jennifer says. "But Way of Life includes religion."

"You can't have my stuff," I say. "Not unless you tell me why."

And Jennifer won't say anything.

But after school I asked her again and she sighed and said, "It's personal. But if I tell you, will you promise to let me have Way of Life?"

"Okay," I say.

"There's this religion in Brazil. It's based on voodoo and practically everybody's into it. I want to know more about it. Anyway, that's why I want to do Way of Life."

"You're into voodoo?" I say. I don't know what that is. I've only heard it's some kind of magical stuff.

"Not yet," Jennifer says. "Maybe someday I'll go down there and study it. Right now I'm just into the Craft."

"What's that?" I ask.

"Witchcraft," Jennifer says.

And then she starts to tell me that the Craft is really just the old religion that got pushed underground. She says she's been a witch for about a year, and she's really lucky because her name is magikal. *Jennifer* means "the white bow" in an ancient language that nobody speaks now, and that the white bow is the crescent moon, and the crescent moon is really the hunting bow of the Goddess, and that witchcraft is really the worship of her. And that is the coolest thing I have ever heard about a name.

"I wonder what my name means," I say.

"You should know," Jennifer says. "Names are part of your power. Want to go look it up?"

And we go to the library and Jennifer shows me this book with everybody's name in it, and it turns out that *Susan* means "lily." Which is lame, because I am not a lily.

But she says, "It's cool. You can make up your own name when you're ready. That's allowed. In fact, it's the best way."

"Did you make up yours?" I ask.

"No," says Jennifer. "I was one of the lucky ones. I got the right name when I was born. But until you discover your true name you can be Lily in rituals."

"What rituals?" I say.

"Want to come to one?" she says, and tells me that there's a new moon this Friday night and do I want to come over to welcome it?

Of course I want to come over and welcome the new moon. So I ask if I can go over to Jennifer's and hang out Friday night.

It's no problem for The Rentz. BD isn't home, and Mommy Angel is happy about it. Because she thinks I must be happy.

Which I am, kind of. But still. No reason for her to go off like a Japanese anime kitty on happy crackers.

She's reading one of her favorite books, the *APEX!* catalog, which is full of stuff nobody needs and only people who own their own computer companies can afford. I tell her I want to go visit my friend, Jennifer. She looks up from the page with the Twin Stainless Steel Maximilian Style Suits of Armor, Perfect for Your Foyer on it, and her eyes light up. She even closes the catalog.

"Oh, it's so good you're beginning to make friends," she says. "High school can be such a drag. I hated it. Go, go, go. Have a wonderful, wonderful time, my darling, and come home happy."

I mean, jeez.

Being happy is very important to Mommy Angel. If someone is not happy, it must be time to go shopping. Mommy Angel goes shopping a lot.

She used to be a nightclub singer. She worked in these really tough places where she had to do songs about love and the moon and love and the stars and love and forever. Then she married BD and stopped working. She still sings, though. Around the house and stuff. I think she wants to crawl into the songs and live in them.

So, anyway, I get to go to Jennifer's.

Jennifer lives close by, but in an apartment, not a house. She's alone when I get there because Jennifer lives with just her mother, and her mother's out. So she's got her altar out in the middle of the living room, and she lets me light the candles and she lights the incense and it is all really cool.

"The New Moon is the best time to ask for something you want," Jennifer says. "Because it's going to be spending the next two weeks growing. So you're more likely to get it."

"What are we doing this ritual for?" I ask.

"For gold," Jennifer says. "My mom and I need more money. So this is a ritual for gold."

And we say a chant that Jennifer has copied out of a book called *The Witche's Formulary of Magick*. And the candlelight is beautiful and the incense smells like roses and I feel like I'm doing something real and powerful. And best of all, I'm doing it with Jennifer.

After that, we did a lot of rituals. Some of them were blessings and to honor the moon or the seasons and stuff like that. The rest were charms and spells for gold.

I never had a friend like Jennifer before.

I loved doing the stuff and I loved learning it. And Jennifer said I was really good at it.

She said, "You know, Lily, you might be better than me at this stuff in a few years. You really get the universe's attention sometimes. I can feel it."

Sometimes she would do stuff for other people, as a secret favor, and I would help. Never *to* other people. Because of the Rule of Three. Whatever bad thing you put on somebody else, you will get back three times as much. That's white magick for you.

I could feel the universe getting bigger and deeper for me.

Then the worst happened. The gold spells worked. Jennifer's mother got engaged to this guy and he gave her this big gold ring. Then they all moved to Kansas City because he'd gotten this great job there. And they got married.

No more Jennifer.

I guess she still misses me. I hear from her once in a while. But there's not much about the Craft in her e-mails. They're mostly about how great her new dad is, or how Kansas City isn't as lame as the name makes you think. She even knows some other witches.

"Kansas City isn't really in Kansas," she texted me a month after she got there. "It's in Missouri. This dislocation gives it an eldritch quality, which draws the Powers. I am gaining strength here. Also, there are more fountains in Kansas City than any place but Rome. TTFN."

Swell.

But I am furious at the universe for answering our charms and spells in such a sneaky way. The universe was selfish to take Jennifer away from me.

What good is a universe if you can't trust it?

BD AND ME

THIS CHAPTER IS MORE ABOUT ME. But in a way it is advice, too.

Back in the days before I met Jennifer, BD and I did compute. I was Daddy's little girl, if you can believe that. I thought he was wonderful and he thought I was right. The fact that he was around maybe six hours a day, tops, just made him more special to me. And when there was that take-your-daughter-to-work-day thing every year, I didn't mind that he never asked me. I just had Mommy Angel drive me over to his business. Because I knew that he was too busy to remember. Then I would sit in the smoky dark and eat ice cream with him all day.

And Mommy Angel thought everything was wonderful, which in a way it was, so she was happy. And if there was a mommy thing to do, she did it with me. I was even in Brownies for a year, and Mommy Angel was my troop leader. She had the uniform and everything. Actually, she had three uniforms. That was her version of Be Prepared.

And when I needed help with my homework, she got me a tutor.

I asked her why she didn't just help me, but she explained: "Oh, honey, I am just not smart enough for all the things you're learning. I mean, thank heaven you have your father's mind, but there's no point in me trying to teach you math. I want you to get the best education there is."

And she got some guy with a PhD to explain prealgebra to me, which is why I am good at algebra.

It was like my whole life came out of a catalog. But that was cool. They were good catalogs.

But after Jennifer and the universe happened, I began to suspect that these people who said they were my parents were actually a couple of aliens from Planet Clueless, and that my real parents were aboard the mother ship somewhere having horrible probes put into them.

Because how could my real parents be so dumb/mean about everything that had started to matter so much to me? But that is the fact. And to prove it, here is the day I learned it.

I had set up an altar in my room, and I was doing spells to get the universe to bring Jennifer back. One day when I was burning some bread to try to get this demon to do me a favor, and BD had stopped at the house to change his shirt, he smelled the smell coming from my room and followed it, and opened my door without even knocking.

HERE'S WHAT HAPPENED

BD: What is going on, Susan?
ME: A ritual. Close the door.

And he did, but he was still on the same side of it I was.

BD: Susan, what are you doing?
ME: I told you. Now go away. This is my room.

And he came over to my altar and saw my stuff and got all bent out of shape.

BD: Susan, is this witchcraft? It is, isn't it?

And he actually knocked everything onto the floor.

ME: Stop it!
BD: No, you stop it. You're stopping it right now. I don't
know where you got these ideas, but you will not
do these things in this house. Good Lord, Susan,
don't you know this nonsense is completely irra-
tional?

(Right. Like sitting in front of a bunch of computers sucking
on tobacco until you fall over from a heart attack is rational.)

BD: It's primitive.

(Right. Like kicking a plate of burning bread onto the floor
isn't primitive.)

BD: It's stupid!

(Unlike intelligently sitting in front of computer screens eating
ice cream until—never mind. Just look back up the page.)

BD: And you will not be involved in it.

(Hello? BD? Guess what? There's religious freedom in this
country. Maybe you didn't get that memo.)

BD: The human race has struggled for centuries to get
beyond these lies, and here you are sucking up this
junk like the scientific revolution never happened.
What's wrong with you?

I am so mad that I want to hit him. But I get control of myself, sort of, and without crying I say:

ME: Daddy, what do you believe in?
BD: Never mind about me.
ME: What do you believe in?
BD: Lots of things.
ME: Like what?

He thinks this one over for a while. Then he says:

BD: I believe in really good software.
ME: Everybody believes in software.
BD: Then everybody's right.
ME: I mean, do you believe in God or the Goddess, or anything?
BD: I don't know. And neither does anybody else.
ME: Well, I believe in this.
BD: Then get over it. Now.

And he stomps out of my room and goes off to work.

HERE IS WHAT HAPPENS NEXT

Mommy Angel is downstairs pretending she doesn't hear anything. Just like she pretended she didn't smell my incense all the times I burned some. After BD leaves, I go downstairs and see her in her favorite place in the living room. She is looking through catalogs for more stuff to buy. She is also singing. It is one of the songs she always sings when she is looking through catalogs.

I don't want diamonds. I don't need pearls.
I just want to be somebody's girl.

It is one of the ancient songs she used to sing in nightclubs. All her songs are ancient. But she has a great voice.

HERE IS WHAT WE SAID

ME: Do you believe in God or anything, Mom?

MA gives this big sigh and looks up with this fakey smile and says:

MA: That's something everyone should decide for themselves, dear.

ME: Well, I decided for *my*self, and Big Daddy just trashed my room for it.

MA: Well, maybe you're a little young to decide for yourself. You're only fourteen.

ME: What have you decided for *your*self?

MA: Oh, I don't know.

ME: You're thirty-eight. When are you going to be old enough to decide?

MA: Susan, how would you like to go shopping?

ME: No.

MA: I'll buy you some new shoes.

ME: I don't want any.

MA: How about a purse?

ME: How about a different father?

MA: Susan, you shouldn't say things like that.

I stomp back upstairs and slam my door.
The End

But even though I was furious and hurt, and The Rentz had been completely unfair, I tried at first to make them see reason. I mean, I knew what the Craft recommended. Rule of Three.

Return good for evil and it will come back to you threefold. I returned good for evil. And I used white magick to do it.

BD had a big contract he was trying to get, so I did seven different good-luck spells to help him. I put charms in his pockets when he was asleep, and sneaked a slide of a mandala into his PowerPoint presentation. I even recorded a ringer for his cell on the night before the big meeting. When it went off, my voice said, "O, Goddess, look with compassion on my Daddy as he tries to score this deal with LunaTech. May his bid be lowest and his technical support the most extensive, and may his software find favor in their sight." Then I called during the meeting to make sure it went off.

Of course he got the contract. And he came home and he thanked me and the universe.

Yeah, right.

Or anyway, two out of three:

He GOT the contract.
He CAME home.
Then: He GROUNDED me for a week, TOOK AWAY
my allowance for two weeks, and told me never to do anything like that again.

"Dammit, Susan, you have embarrassed me in front of my co-workers and my client," he said. "What are you trying to do to me?"

"Help?" I said.

"How is it supposed to help me when a totally irrelevant slide appears in the middle of my presentation?" he hollered. "It threw off the whole sequence of my talk. And when the president of LunaTech asked me what it was, I didn't know what to say. What was that damn thing anyway?"

"A symbol of wholeness," I said.

"Well, it looked like a volleyball," BD said. "And that thing you put on my cell. Thank God the client didn't hear it. As it

was, only Charlie and Ram heard it, and they both laughed so
hard it almost broke up the meeting. So get this straight—no
more spells. No more luck charms or whatever they are. No
more witchcraft in this house—ever. Got it?"

"Speaking of getting things, you're welcome," I said.

"Welcome for what?" he said.

"Welcome for the contract," I said.

And I was grounded for *two* weeks.

THE WITCHCRAFT WAR

THAT WAS THE START of the Witchcraft War.

I never tried to cast a spell in my house again. I did them at night in the backyard. Under the elm tree. And the moon would shine down through its leaves and touch my altar and the powers would be flowing up to it and down to me. And it wasn't white magick anymore, either. Where BD was concerned, I was done with that. If he didn't respect what I had done *for* him, maybe he would respect what I did *to* him.

I didn't care about the Rule of Three. I wanted BD to have to admit that I was right and he was wrong. So I started casting spells for his car to break down and his business to lose money. None of them worked, but that was cool. I'd never worked the dark side before. I figured the universe would have to take a while to shift gears.

Meanwhile, until my skills got stronger, I did other things just to show my male and female alien housemates I wasn't going to be their little girl anymore. I started calling Big Daddy Big Daddy and Mommy Angel Mommy Angel, which they hated. I also called them The Rentz, which they hated even more.

And I kept asking BD and MA the kinds of questions they didn't want to answer. Little things like, "How come I can't believe in something just because you don't?" and "What happens when we die?" Which made Mommy Angel want to take me shopping a lot. Sometimes I'd let her. And I'd get another piercing and an earring to go with it. And green hair.

All of which made BD majorly mad at me. And made MA spend even more time with her catalogs. So I did more of it.

And when Mommy Angel said, "Oh, Susan, why can't you be like you were?" I said, "Why can't you let me be who I am now?"

She just sighed and went back to her catalogs and later I heard her singing real softly:

Oh, my baby, why can't we
Be the way we used to be?
Back when things were soft and light?
Can't it be that way tonight?

And I felt like I'd won a battle.

There was one time when things were a little bit different. For about two minutes. And only with BD. It was the time I said, "I think ghosts are true. I'll bet there are ghosts all over the place and we just don't see them because we have the lights on all the time."

And BD said, "I used to wish I could believe in something like that. I really did. I even tried for a while. I read one of my sister's stupid books about life after death or something. But it was garbage. There's just no evidence."

And I said, "There's lots of evidence. There's evidence for all kinds of things."

"Not scientific evidence," BD said.

"Well, how do you get scientific evidence without experiments?" I said. "What do you want, a haunted laboratory?"

"Yeah," BD said.

"Okay, so you believe in science. I believe in witchcraft. Why can't I believe what I want and you believe what you want?"

"Because I'm right," BD said.

Which explained everything. Except how I got into this family.

Which is why I changed my name to Kestrel. Because a kestrel is a kind of hawk. It's small and it bites and it scratches and it flies high up against the sun and from there it sees ten times better than anyone down on earth. Just like me. And since I couldn't fly, I spent as much time as I could on the roof.

Which is where I was when BD had his heart attack.

I was sitting there with my weeds and my clouds when he drove up. He saw me and shouted at me to get down off the roof and stop smoking. Like Two Blocks Away and They Heard Every Word he shouted.

And I said, "Come on up, Big Daddy. I smoke your brand," and waved the pack at him.

In our front yard we have a walnut tree very good for climbing and walnuts. I could reach the roof that way by climbing out along one long branch that pointed toward the house. Usually I took the bougainvillea, but the tree was just as good.

But if you're forty years old and fat as a Before picture in a weight-loss ad, you shouldn't climb trees.

But that is what Big Daddy did then. He climbed up the tree trying to get to the roof, and me.

His face was red as fire and his eyes were twitching, and even though he wasn't halfway up the tree yet, I backed up all the way to the peak of the roof.

BD was trying to force himself into the crotch of the tree,

grunting and panting, and staring at me, and all of a sudden he fell out.

I was so surprised I laughed. But I didn't want to. And it wasn't funny. Because he lay there on the ground going, "Oh, my God…" and grabbing at his chest.

So I screamed, "Mom!" and she didn't come, and I screamed it again, and she didn't come, and then I just screamed.

And BD sort of crawled to the front door and banged. And then I heard Mommy Angel let out a scream of her own, and in a few minutes I heard the sirens.

And the fire truck came and the ambulance came and the paramedics came and I got down and watched them take BD away on a stretcher with a white sheet over him and a mask on his face so he could breathe.

And I was more scared than I ever knew I could be.

And I swear I never cast any kind of spell for BD to have a heart attack. Never. The universe did that all on its own.

All this is why I know you cannot trust the universe and you have to be able to control it. And if that's black magic, blesséd be.

THE TRUTH

I HAVE TO INTERRUPT THIS GRIMOIRE to write this chapter. I was going to show you how to do an inventory of magick, but that will have to wait.

Because The Rentz called tonight. Actually, it was Mommy Angel. She had her niciest voice on. If niceness was muscles, she'd be a lady wrestler instead of a singer.

HERE'S WHAT WE SAID

MA: Hello, Susan dear.

ME: Sorry, you must have the wrong number.

MA: *Kestrel.* Anyway, I've been trying and trying your cell phone, but I didn't get any answer. Is there something the matter with it?

ME: Not as far as I know.

MA: Then did you get my messages?

ME: I don't know. I turned it off.

MA: But why?

ME: I couldn't think of anybody I wanted to talk to.

MA: Oh.

ME: What do you want?

MA: I want to know how you're doing, of course.

ME: If you really want to know how I'm doing, bring me back home and see for yourself.

MA: We will, dear. Just as soon as your father's heart is strong enough.... Are you and Alice getting along?

ME: Nobody here by that name.

MA: I meant *Ariel*.

ME: She's okay, I guess. Okay?

MA *(Sighing)*: Do you need anything for school?

ME: How about some teachers with brains?

MA: That's not funny, Susan.

ME: I'm not joking, and my name's not Susan.

MA: You haven't asked me about your father.

ME: I haven't asked you about anything.

MA: He's been feeling much stronger.

ME: Ever since I left, right?

MA: Yes. That is, no, not really... Sus—Kestrel, could I please speak to Ali—Ariel?

ME: Can't. She's in the middle of a spell.

MA: A spell. What's the matter with her? Didn't you dial 911?

ME: Not that kind of spell, Mommy Angel. She's casting a love spell for some geek who wants her husband back.

MA: Oh. Of course. I'm sorry, but ever since your father's attack, all I can think of when I hear the word *spell* is—

ME: Whatever.

Then Aunt Ariel comes in from the garage. She's sweaty. It's hot in there. There's some kind of sweet incense smell following her like a lovesick puppy, and she's wearing a caftan with crescent moon pins stuck all over it. All different. There must be about three hundred. Aunt Ariel's body has lots of space for decorations. She looks like a purple Milky Way.

AA: Who is that, Kestrel?
ME: My mom.
AA: How nice. Does she want to speak with me?

I hand her the phone and leave the room. From the living room I listen while I pretend to read my library book, *The Witche's Formulary of Magick*. It is the one Jennifer used, and reading it is a little like being with her again. I am seriously considering stealing it from the library. But witches never steal.

AA: Oh, you're not interrupting at all, Sandra. I've been working in the garage. I'm sweating like a horse. Glad to talk to you. Casting a love spell? That's not quite how I'd put it. Our girl has quite an imagination, hasn't she?… I think she's settling in quite nicely.… Of course she dislikes school. What is there for her to like?… No, anyone who likes high school has a potentially severe personality disorder. Jocks and cheerleaders often never get over their glory years. It's pathetic, really. We wouldn't want that for her. But don't worry; she'll never be that kind.… Oh…the dress code thing is fine. Of course she wasn't happy about it at first, but everything's worked out now. *(Dropping her voice)* I think I've convinced her to give up smoking.… It was nothing. She'd just never considered all the consequences before. *(Voice back up)* She's really wise for someone her age.

She's got that right anyway.

AA: How's my brother?… Good… Good. Yes, he will have to take better care of himself from now on. He should have started doing it years ago…. Maybe six months? No problem. She's welcome here forever. What are family for? Home is the place where, when you have to go there, they have to take you in, as Robert Frost said…. Don't worry about it. You've got enough on your plate with Ted. No, believe me, it's a pleasure…. Yes, I'll get her. Kestrel.

I have to admit, I like the way she calls my name. Like she means it. Like she's not thinking "Susan" when she says it. I go back in and take the phone.

When I pick it up, MA is humming. I know the tune and the words:

I wish we were together
In some cozy little room
Where the flicker from the fire
Chases all my fear and gloom.

MA: S—Kestrel, I am so pleased to talk with you and Ariel. It sounds like you're fitting right in.

ME: That depends on who you talk to.

MA: And I'm so pleased you're quitting smoking. You don't know what a relief that is to me. Your father smoked for years and you see what it's done to him.

ME: Well, I've just got a lot more respect for my aura than he ever had.

MA: Your what?

ME: My aura.

MA: Never mind…. And you're getting along so well with Ariel.

ME: I am? Thanks for telling me.

MA: It seems so long since you left.

ME: Since you threw me out? It sure as hell does.

MA: Kestrel, dear, you know we don't want you to talk like that.

ME: You don't? Damn, I'm sorry.

MA: Darling, if you need anything, just call. Your father and I want you to be as comfortable as you can while you're down there.

ME: Not everyone sees comfort as a goal.

MA: *(Pause)* I suppose that's true.... Goodbye, darling. We'll call again soon.

ME: Whatever.

Click.

The End

I put down the phone. Ariel puts her hand on it and says, "Blesséd be."

I hate those words. So I say, "You lied to her."

"No, I didn't," Ariel says like she's all surprised.

I say, "I told her you were casting a spell, which was true. You came in and said, 'Not exactly.' That was a lie."

"No," Ariel says. "It might have been a lie if you had said it. You cast spells. I rarely do. What I try to do is to help the universe along in the channels it wants to go anyway. And that's what I was doing in the garage. A spell is an attempt to control the universe."

"Like the universe needs your help?" I say.

"Kestrel, did you ever see water flowing across dry ground?" Ariel says. "Did you ever notice how it will run along fine for a minute, and then stop, like it's trying to decide which way to go next? And sometimes it even flows in more than one direction when it finally gets going again? Well, water isn't the only thing that flows like that. And if I can help it to decide what to do, I will. And, yes, maybe the universe does need our help sometimes. After all, we're part of it."

"But you said—"

"I also told her you have an imagination, which is true," Ariel goes on.

"But you said the dress-code thing was working out," I say.

"Isn't it?" Ariel asks.

"Yeah. But you made it sound like—" I say.

"Listen to me, Kestrel," Ariel says. "One of the first things you learn in the Craft is that a witch never lies, right?"

"Right."

"But that doesn't mean you tell the whole truth to every un-enlightened bozo on the bus. The truth is too precious for that."

Ariel sits down at the table and motions for me to join her.

"Now, what do we know about your mother?" she asks me.

"She's all nicey-micey," I say.

Ariel laughs.

"Ever thought about why she's nicey-micey?" she asks.

"No. She just is," I say.

"Your mama's from a little ol' town on Chesapeake Bay in Old Virginia," Ariel says. "Nice is the religion down there. The un-nicest thing your mama ever did in her whole life was to leave home to be a singer. And what kinds of songs does she sing?"

"Real old stuff," I say. "Purple dusks. Green meadows. White cliffs and blue moons."

"Yep. Very pretty songs from years before she was born," Ariel says. "Nice songs. The nicest songs a nicey-micey lady could find."

Ariel reaches out and covers my hand with hers. Which I have to admit feels good.

"Remember, Kestrel. Your mother doesn't really want to know too much about what's going on. Especially right now. She wants to hear that everything's all right. That you're in school and the dress-code thing is working out and you've stopped smoking. And you *are* in school and the dress-code thing *is* working out, and you *have* stopped smoking. So her world is better now. And everything I told her was the truth. But it was truth she could handle."

It makes sense.

"Not everyone is like us, Kestrel," Ariel says. "Not everyone is a seeker. You already know that. But you have to learn how to love the others anyway, from your standpoint as a seeker. And if you work with love as your ground of being, love for the whole imperfect universe, you'll never go far wrong."

I shrug.

INVENTORY

NOW THAT THE PHONE CALL IS OVER and I am back in my room, I will show you how to do your own magick inventory. It is really just lists.

MAGICK I CAN ALREADY DO

1. Make myself vomit by invoking Moloch, with finger backup.
2. Image other realities.
3. Make caterpillars come by singing to them.

(I discovered this power in seventh grade. Three times I called caterpillars to me by singing softly to them and by holding out my finger. They all crawled onto it, and up my arm. If I just held out my finger, they never came. I'm glad to have this power, but I don't know what it's good for.)

4. I can tell what The Rentz are going to say before they say it.

(This power isn't good for anything, either.)

5. Sometimes I dream things before they happen.

(This is definitely the coolest of all my powers so far, but it's not good for anything, either. I never remember the stuff I dreamed until it's already happening. I need to work on this.)

6. Make someone I hate leave early by opening a pair of scissors and pointing it at them in another room.

(The Rentz had a party last year and made me go to bed early. So I put out the scissors and everybody left by eleven. It was cool.)

Here is another list you need to keep. It is not as good as the first list, but it is just as important.

MAGICK I TRIED THAT DIDN'T WORK

1. Turning my allowance into gold.

(One week I got my allowance changed into dollar coins and cast this spell. I figured since the dollars were gold-colored already that would help. But it didn't.)

2. Turning my ice skates into gold.

(Same spell.)

3. Turning the silverware into gold.

(Different spell.)

4. Conjuring the spirit of Sir Isaac Newton to do my math homework.
5. Conjuring any spirit to do my math homework.

6. Putting a spell on Ms. Larsen, my math teacher, so that she would stop giving homework.
7. Seeing fairies.
8. Talking to the dead with a tape recorder.
9. Looking into a mirror in a room lit only by a black candle to see who I had been in a previous life.
10. Reading tarot cards.
11. Making a voodoo doll of Ms. Larsen.

That's my inventory. Maybe a hundred years from now everybody will be able to do things like this. Maybe not. But if they are, it will be because people like me led the way. I hope they appreciate it.

Because I will keep trying. And I don't care what Ariel says about water flowing. They put dams and levees on rivers, and when they break, it's a disaster. People drown. Buildings get crushed. Towns get wiped out. That's what can happen when water makes up its mind.

THE UNIVERSE GETS MORE BOGUS

IT IS MORE THAN A WEEK since I wrote my inventories and I am still here. I continue to develop my powers, but the universe doesn't care. I would have to say it doesn't give a damn, actually.

While I wait for it to bend to my will, I am going to my classes and doing my homework and getting okay grades.

I have a nickname now. I'm The Girl Who Doesn't Wear the Uniform. Catchy.

And nobody talks to me, which is cool, because what do pigeons have to say to a kestrel anyway? I'm lonely, but I'm not lonely for these sucky unenlightened bozos with their teams and clubs and marching band.

I want Jennifer to come back. I want a coven. I want to be with my own kind.

To remind myself of who I really am, I copied a pentagram out of *The Witche's Formulary of Magick* and taped it to the back of my locker. I can look at it every time I open the door. It is like a quick drink of water to see it.

And then, today, because the universe doesn't have anything better to do than make things worse for me, it does.

This morning my locker has the word EVIL written on it in black marker. Okay, that's cool. But when I open the locker the same thing is written on the inside. That is gigantically creepy because no one but me is supposed to be able to get into my locker, right?

And written on the front cover of my algebra book is GET OUT OF OUR SCHOOL WITCH. And on the back cover is YOU'RE AUNT'S A SATAN. And on the front cover of my English book is U R DAMED. That's crossed out and DAMMED is written under it. And on the back is STOP CASTEING SPELLS.

I take everything out of my locker and stuff it into my backpack. No way am I going to leave anything here to be messed with again. But when I stand up, my backpack weighs about ten thousand pounds.

Nobody said it's easy being a witch.

I start trying to figure out how to cast spells on people when you don't know exactly who they are. This is a hard question and probably explains what happens next.

When I get to my algebra class, I sit down without looking. Big mistake. Because there is a tack on the seat. The only thing lamer than putting a tack on a seat is not noticing it. I blame the universe, because if I hadn't been thinking about who trashed my stuff and how to curse them, I would have noticed it.

So, like a dork, I sit on the tack and say, "Oww!" and jump up, and pull it out of my butt.

And the whole class laughs.

"Score!" shouts a girl.

And this is a surprise, because it is Tiffany Holmer, one of the Queens, which is this in-in group of about five girls who think they were born to rule the planet and are practicing with the ninth grade. And Amber Williams, who is one of the other Queens, giggles.

My private name for them is T&A. But they don't know that. No one knows that. But I am now clearly on their to-do list.

I am so mad I can't even open my mouth. But I have to do something. So I wave my hand slowly, making it look like I'm doing some kind of magickal spell, and then I point straight at Tiffany. Then I sit down.

Anyway, we then spend a fascinating fifty minutes finding out all about x over y times n. (I have to say, if algebra was good for anything, it would be interesting. If x minus y over quantity m minus n equaled Your Bra Strap Breaks You Queen Pig, I would be an A student.) Then the bell sends us out of the room and I head for gym.

I am a little surprised to find that no one has done anything nasty to my gym rags, but no one has, and I go out and do jumping jacks and girls' push-ups.

It is when I get out of the shower that I find out what my new friends have been doing.

My stuff is gone. All of it. No clothes, no backpack. Even my sweaty gym stuff is gone. What I have is a small wet towel. And a note where I left my stuff. Which says:

NEED CLOTHES? CASTE A SPELL.

A Witch Never Complains, but what am I supposed to do? Ms. Stendahl, who is head coach because she once won an Olympic medal in stove-tossing, comes in. I tell her.

She blows her whistle and hollers, "Who took this girl's stuff?"

Of course everyone rushes to confess.

So Ms. Stendahl has everyone dump out their backpacks. But the ones who did it got out fast before I could find out what they'd done. So no one has anything of mine.

So Ms. Stendahl says she's going to have roll call again.

"We'll be late for class," one of the girls bleats.

"Too bad," Ms. Stendahl says. "I'm going to find out who did this."

"It was Tiffany and Amber," one girl says, and everyone looks at her. Because, of course, you do not tell on a Queen.

"Oh, Laura," someone says. "Oh, man."

"So can we go to class now?" Laura asks. "I have a test."

"Thanks," Ms. Stendahl. says. "But I'm still going to take attendance."

Which she does and finds out that—guess what?—Tiffany and Amber are the only ones missing. She lets the other girls go.

I wonder who this girl is who wailed on T&A. I never noticed her before. She's tiny and delicate, and if a mouse was in ninth grade it would look a lot like her. I mean, nothing there. But for some reason she did this. Maybe it was just to try to get to class on time. Probably it was. But maybe she did it for me. But why?

But that takes maybe one second to wonder. What I am wondering the rest of the time is how I am going to get un-naked.

Ms. Stendahl takes me into the office and gets me two dry towels. Then she calls Garbage and tells him what happened.

And here is what happens next:

To me: Aunt Ariel comes down and brings me some clothes. And thanks Ms. Stendahl. And takes me to Garbage's office.

To T&A: NOTHING.

Because by the time we get to Garbage's office, they are just leaving. They are coming out of the door as we are coming down the hall and Tiffany gives us a fakey smile and Amber giggles and they almost run away.

"They're the ones," I say.

Aunt Ariel is like a dog on a tight chain. But when she says, "Let's hear what Mr. Gorringe has to say for himself" her voice is calm and smooth. So calm and smooth it's scary.

The secretary makes us wait maybe half an hour. Finally, she lets us in to see Garbage.

He sighs when we come in.

"And how may I help you today, Ms. Murphy?" he says to Ariel.

"You can begin by helping me to recover my niece's stolen

property," Aunt Ariel says. "And by telling me what punishment you have in mind for the thieves."

"Well, let me begin by saying we have a zero-tolerance policy here at RMN," Garbage says, making a little temple with his fingers. (Maybe that is his fake spell.) "So if, in fact, any thievery has occurred, the perpetrators will be dealt with accordingly."

"So the fact that my niece was left in your locker room dripping wet and naked is, in your mind, *questionable?*" Ariel asks.

"Of course not," Garbage says. "The question is whether the facts are as they appear to be."

"Go on," Aunt Ariel says.

"It is possible that your niece's things have been stolen," Garbage says. "It is also possible—unlikely, but possible—that they have been mislaid. And it is even possible that she may have been involved in their disappearance."

"So she stole her own things to get these girls in trouble. Is that what I hear you saying?" Aunt Ariel's voice is softer now.

Garbage nods. "That is one of the possibilities."

"And she did this while she was in the shower," Aunt Ariel says.

"I do not say when she did it," Garbage says. "I do not say that she did it at all. I must point out, however, that the girls, whom I have just questioned, come from excellent families. They are hardly likely to have stolen anything."

"Whereas my niece comes from a less excellent family, is that correct?" Aunt Ariel says.

Garbage shrugs. One shoulder.

"I did not say that. Let me restate that the girls you are accusing come from *excellent* families."

"Thank you for clearing that up for me," Aunt Ariel says. "Now let me make something clear to you. This school stands *in loco parentis.* I assume you know what that means?"

"Of course," Garbage says.

"Then you are aware that, under the law, you are responsible for her safety from the time she enters the building in the morning until she returns home," Aunt Ariel says. "And your failure to do that today opens you to several possibilities. Including lawsuits and charges of child endangerment."

Garbage stands up. I'm not sure if he's scared or angry or both.

"When people with attitudes like you bring children into the public schools there are bound to be problems," he half shouts, half squeaks. "You need to take responsibility for yourselves."

"I'm not sure I understand the point you're trying to make," Aunt Ariel says.

"The point is, many people find your niece's behavior…provocative and abnormal," Garbage says.

"It sounds, Mr. Gorringe, as if you are belittling our religion."

"You don't have a religion," Garbage shouts. "It's a cult. A satanic cult."

Right then Garbage's secretary knocks on the door.

"Excuse me," she says. "But I think we have a solution to the mystery."

She sort of shoves the girl named Laura into the office. Laura is holding my backpack. She is so small she is almost hidden behind it.

"Hey," she says in a whisper. "I found your stuff."

"Where was it?" I ask.

"In the bushes in front of the school," she says. "Under Mr. Gorringe's window."

"Hah!" says Garbage.

"How did you come to be looking there, dear?" Aunt Ariel asks.

But Garbage says, "I will not allow you to interrogate my students. Open the bag, Ms. Murphy, and see that everything is there."

So I open it, and everything is there, including my stinky gym clothes, which are soaking into the paper covers on my books.

Aunt Ariel holds the algebra book up.

"What's all this?" she asks me.

So I tell her. And about the words on my locker.

"I see," Aunt Ariel says. "And how soon will you have my niece's locker repainted, Mr. Gorringe?"

"By the end of the week," he shrugs.

"I think by tomorrow would be much better," Aunt Ariel says. "I understand you have a *zero-tolerance policy* at this school."

"We'll take care of it as quickly as we can," Garbage says. "And now I think we're done here."

"Only for the moment," Aunt Ariel says. "Kestrel, do you want to go come home, or go back to class for the rest of the day?"

I would love to go home. But that would be what T&A want. To know they got to me. So I say, "Nah. I'll stick around."

"You still have your cell?" Aunt Ariel says.

I show it to her and turn it on.

"If anything more happens, call me at once."

"We're done here," Garbage repeats.

Meanwhile, Laura is standing there looking like a rope that's getting twisted tighter and tighter. She's scared, and I know why. T&A know by now that she told Ms. Stendahl what they'd done. So they threatened her to make her "find" the backpack. Goddess knows what they told her they'd do to her. For that matter, they might do it anyway.

"Hey," I say to her. "That was cool, what you did."

She gives me a little mouth twitch that wants to be a smile.

"Thanks," she says, and skitters away.

THE UNIVERSE REALLY BITES

IT'S SIXTH PERIOD and I'm sitting in class thinking, *If I can get through to the end of the week, maybe they'll get distracted over the weekend and go on to somebody else.* But I know better. Queens may have the attention spans of houseflies for most things, but on some subjects they are like the snow-white, red-eared hounds of the Moon Goddess. One of those subjects: being mean.

Laura looks like she thinks she's still in for it, too. She sits with her head down and her fingers tight around her pen. She doesn't raise her eyes, or pay any attention.

Not that there's anything to pay attention to. The teacher is a grammar freak. Ms. Southworth has just started teaching high school after eight thousand years teaching seventh and eighth grades. She taught grammar there, and she's going to teach it here. Since my schools up north started teaching it in sixth grade, this is the fourth year in a row I have had grammar. Gerunds. Participial phrases. All seventy-two prepositions. I do not know why some ancient goobers sat down and made all this stuff up, but I know it all already. A witch should know it. Grammar = gramarye, after all.

So I am imaging. This is when you imagine yourself at the center of the universe and then imagine there is a great big tree running all up and down it with its branches everywhere, and then you imagine everything in the universe is on the tree like old-time Christmas presents, and you imagine for yourself the things you want the tree to give you.

But it's hard to image what I want. Because it isn't an object.

"Hey, universe," I keep saying in my head. "Lighten up. If you want to diss somebody, diss the Queens. In fact, kill them for me."

Now *that* I can image. T&A hanging from a branch of the tree by their necks. It's a beautiful night and the birds are singing on the other branches. And T&A are slowly twisting back and forth like a couple of dangling participles.

But the universe is not done with dissing me for the day. And when the next bad thing happens, it doesn't come from the Queens. It comes from José Iturrigaray and Blake Cump, who not only are not subjects of the Queens, they don't even hang together with each other. Which only proves the universe is ganging up on me.

It is the end of the day and I am taking my pentagram down because they are going to paint my locker, right?

My locker is in the second row of them next to my English class, which José Iturrigaray is in, even though he's a year older than any other kid there, and he looks big enough to be in college—or in state prison, which is where he really belongs.

He always comes into class late, and he always wears shades even when the teacher turns out the lights and shows a video to enrich our understanding of pronouns or adverbs while she does whatever it is teachers do when they're not teaching and they're supposed to be. He always slouches like he's hoping somebody's going to drop a nickel that he can dive for. His face never moves.

And every day at 2:25 p.m. this cherried-out deep blue '57 Chevy covered with more chrome than they mine in Africa in two years and riding three inches off the ground pulls up rumbling and purring like a tiger, and the back door opens. José gets in with three guys who look just like him, except they are older and they all look like they are carved out of granite, and they peel out. I don't know where they take him. Maybe they put him back in his coffin and he comes out again at midnight.

No, if that were true, there'd be something about him that I could like.

So I'm kneeling in front of my locker and I hear this voice behind me and it says, "How come you don't wear the uniform?"

I turn around and there's José. The slouch. The glasses. The no-move face.

"Because it sucks," I say.

"Everybody else got to wear it," he says.

"Because everybody else sucks," I say.

"How come you got that thing in there?" he says.

By *that thing* I know he means my sacred pentagram.

I think, *A Witch Never Lies. But what truth can he handle?*

While I'm still thinking, he says, "Is it satanic?"

"Oh, man," I say. "We've been getting that bogus rap laid on us for a thousand years. No, it's not satanic. And it's not *Titanic,* either. It's just part of my religion, okay?"

"What religion's that?" he asks.

"Never mind. I don't want to talk about it," I say.

"You a witch?" he asks me.

By now there's this cluster of kids standing around to listen to us. They probably never knew José could talk before. And one of those kids is Blake Cump. I'd say Blake has a face like a perverted rat, but that would be an insult to all the perverted rats in the world. He's also in English. José never talks. Blake never shuts up.

"A witch!" he shouts. "Blondie's a witch! Aaaah!"

Never call me Blondie. Never call me Susan. Never call me Blondie.

"Shut up!" I say.

"Ooh, Blondie's gonna turn me into a *newt!*" Blake shouts, and everybody else starts laughing. They're not laughing because he's funny. They're laughing because they see he's getting to me and they want me to lose it.

"Somebody already beat me to it," I shout back.

"Ooh, the witch told a joke. Blondie told a joke. Hey, that's her name. Blondjoke."

I'm on my feet now, my back's to my locker, and I hear a sound behind me. I turn around, and somebody's ripped my pentagram out of my locker and is running down the hall with it.

I scream and start after them. But somebody blocks my way. Somebody else dumps my backpack. Out falls *The Witche's Formulary of Magick.*

"Ooh, satanic," somebody shouts.

"Cool!" says Blake and starts off with it under his arm.

"Give that back! It isn't mine, it's the library's," I say, and I start after Blake.

This time, instead of blocking me, somebody trips me. I fall and bite my tongue. I start to get up and see blood on the linoleum.

"Ew, gross," says one of the more sympathetic pigs.

I'm surrounded by blue uniform legs, and everyone's laughing except someone who's shouting, "A witch, a witch, a Blondjoke witch. Hey, you better cast a spell on that tongue."

I can't talk. My tongue hurts like fire, and I'm scared, mad, and crying. Then the legs start to move. Fast. And they're gone. And there's this teacher standing there who helps me up and takes me in the teachers' lounge and puts some ice on my tongue, which is the pits, but eventually the bleeding stops.

He asks who I want him to call, but I just shake my head. I

want to walk home. I want some privacy. I go down the quiet hall and out onto the street, which is also quiet now. Everyone else was picked up long ago.

Every step of the way home I'm working out the spells I'm going to cast on Blake Cump and José Iturrigaray.

9

THE UNIVERTH THUCKTH

WHEN I GET HOME, I have to write out what happened, because I can't talk. Aunt Ariel stands over me like a thunderstorm waiting to happen.

She gets on the phone to Garbage the next morning and there is a LONG conversation. The outcome is, José and Blake get detentions for a while, and Gorringe will get my book back from Blake. It doesn't sound like much to me.

Anyway, I'm off school until I can talk again. It gives me a chance to see what Ariel does all day.

Aunt Ariel used to have a real job. A lot of real jobs, I think. I used to hear BD say things like "You'll never believe what that idiot sister of mine is up to now" after their annual talk on the phone.

Aunt Ariel always calls BD on the day before his birthday. Not calling him the rest of the year is supposed to be his present.

Anyway, whatever she did before, she's into desktop publishing now. She does a newsletter called *Grimoire*. *Grimoire* is full of articles on how to grow your own mugwort and how to image white light more successfully. The rest is full of personals and lame poems. Most of it is written by other witches she pays in copies of the newsletter and herbs from her garden. Thousands of people send her money for this thing every year, and she gets invited to speak to women's groups and libraries about being a witch and she gets paid for that, too.

I'd like to do that. Maybe after I've afflicted Blake and José with incurable pustulent boils over every part of their bodies and the Queens are run over by a garbage truck, I'll be invited to libraries to tell how I did it.

Anyway, incurable pustulent boils are my new interest. They are my first step in my campaign of revenge. I plan to go on from there, but I know I'll have to work up to it slowly. Really nasty spells take a lot of practice.

Ariel's office is in one of the bedrooms. Besides her 'puter and her printer and her scanner and stuff, she has her books. Two whole walls, and all on the Craft. Some of them aren't even in English. I figure the spell I want has got to be in one of them, but how will I find it? I know she won't tell me. Not Ms. White Magick Only.

So this morning I go in there and just kind of browse. Way up at the top of the shelves is *The Alembic of the Soul.* Next to it is *Yeats As Magician. The Herbalist's Compendium. Die Untedrückerung Die Hexerei in Deutschland in XVI Jahrhundert.*

I pull down this one and try to figure out what it's about. The printing isn't even something I can recognize. It stares back at me like a lot of fat little wiggly uglies under a microscope. A few letters look something like the English alphabet, but even these have spikes and horns all over them. How can anybody read this stuff?

Ariel comes and stands in the doorway with a cup of coffee in her hand. I don't know if I'm allowed in here or not. She never said.

"Onh. Hni," I say with the book in my arms.

"It's all right, Kestrel," Aunt Ariel says. "I don't mind you looking through my library. What are you reading?"

"Thinh," I say. "Inh looks inneresthinh. Whanh inh ih?"

Ariel takes the book and says, "Oh. *The Suppression of Witchcraft in Germany in the Sixteenth Century.*"

"You cah reah thih?"

"I wouldn't have bought it if I couldn't read it," Aunt Ariel says. "Cost me an arm and a leg. But money spent on a book you want is never wasted."

I go on looking at the titles. If Aunt Ariel has read them all, she must be the smartest witch on the planet.

So I ask, "Havh you reah all theth?"

"Most of them," Aunt Ariel says. "Sometimes I buy books in the hopes I'll grow into them."

"Gool," I say.

Then she says, "Were you looking for anything in particular?"

I start to lie. Then I remember A Witch Never Lies.

"A thpell," I say. "Thomethig tho dho tho thoth guyth."

"That ol' black magic?" Ariel says. "Don't mess with it if you want to grow into your own powers, Kestrel. It will always lead away from them, even if it works. Especially if it works. And it always comes back at you. That's its nature."

"But they *hurgh* me."

"Yes. And their punishment isn't very much," Aunt Ariel said. "And as for those girls—" She shakes her head. "Gorringe."

Then she sits down in a big armchair she has in there. It's big enough for two people, even when one of them is her. She pulls me down beside her and puts her arm around me. It's big, soft, and warm, like the chair. "Why do you suppose the universe is letting them off so lightly?"

"Cauth the univerth thuckth," I say.

"Think about it, Kestrel. You bit your tongue. The universe is trying to tell you to be careful what you say. The Craft isn't for everybody. The universe is using them to tell you that." Ariel hugs me harder.

"Buht I didnh't thay anythinh to the Queenth," I say. "And Jothé athked me. Whath wath I thupposedh to dho?"

"The Queens are a problem, all right," Aunt Ariel says. "But you're a problem for them, too. Just by being yourself you challenge their power. And they see you as a great threat, even though you don't care about them one way or the other. *Because* you don't care. But let's work with José and Blake. What would you say if it were that moment again and you could live it over?"

I tell her what I would say and she laughs. It must sound really funny with my mouth the way it is.

"Well, that's straightforward and concise," she says. "But not very original. What would you really say? Take your time. You're making up an answer that will serve you for the rest of your life. Because we both know there will be other Josés."

I think hard. I image it. I see José's face, his stupid, blank face. Those glasses of his. I don't know what to say to him. Then I see Blake, looking ready to gnaw me. What can you say to someone like Blake?

Then it comes to me. "Whath a withch?" I say.

Aunt Ariel claps her hands. "Great! Now, what do they say?"

I go back into my image. José isn't saying anything. But Blake can't keep his mouth shut to save his life.

"You ride on a broomstick?" he asks me.

I say this out loud, then I answer, "Dho you?"

My mind starts to go real fast and I get quiet.

You cast spells on people? Blake says.

Do you? I thinksay.

You put frogs and stuff in boiling pots? Blake asks.

Do you?

I ain't no witch, Blake finally says.

Cool, I thinksay.

The Blake in my image looks confused. He wants to hurt me, but he can't think how. Then he grins.

"Blondjoke," he says.

I stiffen. This is what I can't defend myself against. That kind of stupidity that's proud of itself. But at least I've defended the Craft. Maybe the universe is helping me out a little, giving me a false identity to help protect who I really am. I don't like it, but it might be true.

I look around. I see José. His arms cross. He shakes his head slowly, like a statue trying to come to life. His lips move. I hear words. He says, "Don't call her…"

And the image breaks.

"Where have you been?" Aunt Ariel asks me.

"Thcool."

"What did you learn there?" Ariel asks.

I tell her what I imaged, and my idea about Blondjoke.

"Buht thahs really lame evenh if ihs thrue," I say. "The univerth thtill thucks."

"Kestrel," says Aunt Ariel. "There's something very important you need to learn about the universe. It isn't black and white. It's black and white."

"Hunh?" I say.

"You know my garage door?" she says. "With the little bit of black in the middle of all that white, and the little bit of white in all that black? That's the nature of the universe. That's the nature of human life. The light and the dark work together even when they're opposing each other. And if you can recognize that, you'll be much more powerful. Instead of taking sides entirely with one or the other, which you can't really do anyway, try this—the next time the universe does something you don't like, image stepping back. Then think, 'That's interesting,' and wait. You may see something surprising."

I don't say anything. I don't have anything to say, and besides, my mouth is tired. But I am surprised. I thought Ariel was just a white witch. Now she says she's something different. I don't know what to call her, exactly. But it might be interesting to find out.

MAJIX

My mouth is a lot better now. I can stop writing words with all those extra letters.

I spend a lot of time alone in my room thinking about the Craft and about how black and white go together and how they don't. Like water. Sometimes it's one thing, sometimes it's another. It can save your life, it can drown you. But it's the same thing either way.

But I'm still not some little wiccan wannabe. I'm a *witch*. I have to find my own path without turning into Tinkerbell or Darth Vader.

I go back into Ariel's office and look at all those books. Every one of them is something about the Craft. Every one of them has something in it I need to know. But how did all that stuff get into those books in the first place? Then it comes to me. Unless every one of those books is a rewrite of all the others, and they all trace back to the first grimoire, they all have to be what one person found out working on her own.

It's like the sun comes up again, right there in that room. It's

MY universe-given powers that make me what I am. I don't need *The Witche's Formulary of Magick,* or anything in this room to become myself. I have to find my own way, and I will write my own book while I do it.

My book of my own powers, which I will call *MAJIX.*

This book. Which I'm already doing.

Maybe the universe was leading me here all along. Maybe I started the book so that *right now* I would realize that I was already on my own path.

I am so jazzed by this idea that I start jumping up and down like a little kid, until my tongue starts to hurt again.

Then I calm down and get this grimoire. I flip back to the places where I wrote MAGICK, cross it out, and write MAJIX.

Then at the bottom of MAJIX I CAN ALREADY DO, I write

7. Step back and say "That's interesting."

Then I start a new inventory.

THINGS I NEED TO WORK ON

1. Starting a coven.
2. Getting a familiar.

(In case you're reading this a hundred years from now and don't know what that is, it's an animal companion. It understands you, and it can spy for you and things. Very good to have, but not required. Ariel doesn't have one.)

3. Getting even with the Queens.
4. Getting even with Blake Cump.
5. Getting even with José, but not as bad.

(I have decided that he's just stupid. Blake's really bad. And detention isn't enough for what they did to me. I just won't use black magick to get them.)

6. Destroying Richard Milhous Nixon Union High.

I turn back to look at the majix I've already developed. Only imaging seems like it's going to be of much help.

I turn off the light. I pull down the shades. I compose myself into the lotus position. I open my mind to allow the images to come.

I guess I must fall asleep, because the next thing I know, my neck hurts and I am jerking my head up because a phone is ringing, and I know I've been dreaming, but the only thing I remember is a man's voice, saying, "Just remember, never write a check with your mouth that you can't cover with your ass."

Then Aunt Ariel is knocking on my door.

"Kestrel, it's Laura from school," she says. "Do you want to talk to her?"

Why would she be calling me? Why would anybody? I am so curious I go pick up the phone.

"Hey," I say.

"Hey," Laura says. "I heard about your tongue. I just wondered if you were okay."

"Kind of," I say. "It doesn't hurt much anymore."

"Hey, listen, do you want me to bring you any homework?" Laura says.

I'm going to say, "Not much." But then I think, maybe she's cool. Anyway, maybe I should find out. I take a step back and thinksay, *Interesting.* Then I really say, "Whatever. If it's no trouble. I'll be back pretty soon. But yeah. Thanks."

"Okay."

Then there's dead air between us. I wonder what more she wants me to say. Or what she wants to say that she isn't saying.

So I say, "Want me to do a protection spell for you?"

She says, "How does that work?"

"I just do a spell and it keeps the Queens off your back," I say. "If it works. I've never done one before so I don't know if it's one of my powers or not."

"Sure," she says. "Please."

"Okay, I'll get on it," I say.

"Thanks," she says.

"Yeah. Well, thanks for the homework."

We hang up.

Aunt Ariel is in her office, just reading in her big chair. I'll bet she came in here to give me and Laura privacy. Cool.

"Aunt Ariel, how do I do a protection spell?" I say. "Laura needs one."

"Just Laura? Not you?" Ariel says.

"Nah. I'm all right," I say. "But I'm a little worried about her."

Aunt Ariel smiles. Then she nods and says,"Worried about somebody else, are we? Come with me."

Aunt Ariel puts on her purple moons robe. We go out to the garage. She lights the candles in the sconces. The shadows flicker on the two-by-fours and the concrete floor and the hot, dark garage turns into a magickal place. Well, duh. That's what it is.

"You don't have anything of Laura's do you?" Aunt Ariel says. "Protection spells require that."

"No," I say.

"Then we'll have to wing it," Aunt Ariel says. "We'll just try to help the universe to decide which way to flow."

"But we'll cast a circle," I say.

"Of course," Ariel says. "What did you think?"

Majix, I think. *This will be majix.*

Aunt Ariel ducks down behind her altar and comes up with a container of salt, a sort of water bottle with holes in the top, a candle, and a bundle of sage.

"Ready to rock and roll," she says. "Kestrel, cast the circle."

I take the salt and I trace over the circle at the center of the pentagram painted on the floor. Salt is very purifying. Also, it's of the earth, which is important.

Meanwhile, Ariel says, "Powers of the universe, we summon you to guard and ward this place. Powers of the universe, we invite you to join our rites. Powers of the universe, we invoke your help for our friend, Laura. Bestow then on our work your blessing, for we intend no bad thing. Blesséd be."

"Which way is north?" I ask.

Ariel points and I set the salt container down in that direction.

"Powers of earth, be Guards of the North," I say.

Ariel lights the candle and hands it to me. Then she lights the sage off it.

"Powers of the universe, we invoke your help for our friend, Laura," I say again. I set the candle down on the south side of the circle. "Powers of fire, be the Guards of the South," I say.

Ariel has lit the sage off the candle and is waving it around. Little ghosts of smoke are trailing out of it.

I sneeze.

"Blesséd be," Aunt Ariel says. "Powers of the universe, we invoke your help for our friend, Laura."

When there's a good cloud of smoke, she sets the sage on the eastern side of the circle and says, "Powers of wind, be the Guards of the East."

Then she hands me the sprinkler thing. I wave it around, making little drops of water fly everywhere.

"Powers of the universe, we invoke your help for our friend, Laura." I set the sprinkler down and say, "Powers of water, be the Guards of the West."

Then Ariel and I take each other's hands, making a circle within the circle.

"Be this circle unbreakable by hate and malice," Ariel says. "Be it eternal, as is its nature. Be it as large as Laura's life, that she may be kept safe within. Blesséd be. Kestrel, is there anything you'd like to add?"

"Yeah," I say. "Hey, universe, this kid's good people. You can't expect people to be good very much if you don't protect them when they are. So keep the Queens off her back. We can do this one of two ways, universe. Either you just keep everything flowing nice and calm around her, or I'll come back to you and work some black magick on the Queens. So if you don't want to be responsible for more bad energy flying around down here, pay attention. That's it."

Ariel says, "May the unbroken circle be cast wide as the world now. May it release us from its bonds, but hold us in loving protection until we call and cast again. Blesséd be."

"Blesséd be," I say, trying hard to mean it.

Ariel blows out the candle and crushes the burning sage. The smell of it gets even stronger. I inhale and smile. It feels good and powerful.

Without talking to each other, we put everything back under the altar. Ariel blows out the candles on one side of the garage. I do the other. We go back in the house.

Ariel wriggles out of her purple robe and smiles.

"You know, sometimes casting the circle gives me the darnedest appetite," she says. "Let's go out to dinner. You pick where."

Dinner out is righteous. Maybe the universe is on my side after all.

ORTHOGONIAN OF THE WEEK

I AM OFF A COUPLE MORE DAYS. Laura brings me my homework and I do it. She doesn't hang around or anything. Her mom or somebody is waiting in the car.

Today, when I get back to school, I run into Laura hanging by the main entrance.

"Did you cast the spell?" she says.

"It's done," I say. "My aunt helped."

"What did you do?" Laura asks.

I shrug. The Craft is not for everybody.

"Well, thanks," she says. "I hope it works."

"The Queens better hope it works," I say. "What we did was white magic. But if the universe lets you down, I'm going to lay some major curses on those slutcakes."

Laura laughs. "Slutcakes! I love it."

I check Laura out, thinking something over. It's hard to tell what she's really like in her little uniform. She seems like a goody. But maybe she's just anxious to be liked. To have me like her. And maybe when she's not trying so hard to be liked, she's a gutsy got-your-back girl. The kind of kid who'd rat out a couple of Queens for you. Maybe.

Step back. Thinksay, *Interesting*.

And I say, "You interested in the Craft?"

She gets all serious and says, "Yes."

"I'm starting a coven," I say. "Maybe I could take you on. If you're interested, meet me after sixth period. We have to talk about some things. And look up your name at the library."

"Okay!" she says.

Then the bell rings and we go off to our homerooms.

The rest of this chapter is about how I do not meet Laura after school or start my coven today and what happens instead.

Every Friday morning Richard Milhous Nixon Union High School has Spirit Assembly. This could be really cool if any spirits showed up, but all it means is that we get pushed into rows by classes in the auditorium and some kid with a trumpet tries to find a bugle call he's supposed to know. Then the band plays the school song, which we are supposed to sing and no one does. Here's how it goes:

What a friend we have in Richard
Milhous Nixon Union High
Where we learn and study gaily (I am not making this up.)
And we'll love it 'til we die.

When at last we go to college
And leave RMN behind,
We'll remember it so fondly
Wherever our trail may wind.

We will always be good students,
Learn by lecture and by book
And we'll tell the whole world proudly,
"World, I am not a crook."

Dr. Garbage wrote it himself. What a surprise.

If you are reading this a hundred years in the future, maybe you need some background now. I didn't get the last line until Aunt Ariel explained to me that it was something Richard Milhous Nixon said back when he was president. Before he had to resign. Because everybody found out he was, in fact, a crook.

You also need to know that the kids who go here are called Orthogonians, which is the name of some club that Richard Milhous Nixon founded when he was in college because he couldn't get into the club he wanted. And get this part: *Orthogonians* means Straight Shooters. The football team is the Fighting Orthogonians. The marching band is the Marching Orthogonians. The school paper is *The Orthogonian Express.* You need to know this because of what comes next at Spirit Assembly. The Awards Ceremony.

Every week, some kid who has been the most helpful to Garbage, like say by ratting out some other kid who was writing on the walls or something, gets this big gold-colored trophy in genuine plastic. He then becomes the official Orthogonian of the Week for the next week. He gets free lunch tickets and is allowed to leave an hour early on Friday.

This week the official Orthogonian of the Week is Blake Cump.

Yeah, right. The same one who got detention for what he did to me. He told Garbage some kids in the boys' bathroom had cigarettes. After they wouldn't give him any.

Garbage makes the same speech he makes every week about how Your-Name-Here exemplifies the highest ideals of Richard Milhous Nixon Union High School (come to think of it, Blake probably does) and he gives him the trophy. And Blake is up there grinning like it's this big joke, and he's right, it is, because even Garbage has to know what really happened.

Blake's friends out in the assembly holler, "Way to go,

Blake!" and he shakes the trophy over his head like a wrestler, while the kids he ratted on holler, "Bogus!" and "Blake sucks!"

So Gorringe blows his whistle, and the teachers all start blowing their whistles and telling us to shut up whether we're making noise or not, and we herd back to our classrooms, and that's all the school spirit for this week.

In English, which is last period, I am surprised to see that Blake is there. But he is, with his trophy. He's filled it with wads of paper and put it by his desk as a wastebasket.

José is also there, acting like I'm not, which is good because that's the way he is with everybody else.

So we're diagramming sentences like it was important, and I have my head bent over my paper and my backpack hung on the back of my chair. I've got my hands over my ears, and when Blake jumps up and starts shouting, it's like his voice is coming from far away.

"Somebody stole my wallet!" He's standing up, feeling in all his pockets and turning around. "My wallet's gone."

Ms. Southworth says, "What does it look like?"

"It looks like a wallet," Blake says. "You know. Flat. Narrow. Brown." He starts to cry. "It had my lunch tickets in it."

"Has anyone seen Blake's wallet?" Ms. Southworth asks.

We all look around our desks like it's somehow migrated from Blake's seat.

"Who's got my wallet?" Blake cries.

Then I feel the straps on my backpack move. I hear the zipper unzip.

Jason Horspool jumps up from the seat behind me and shouts, "Is this it?"

"Yeah, man," Blake says. "Give it here."

"Where was it?" Ms. Southworth says.

"In her backpack," says Jason.

I feel my stomach turn over, my skin get hot, and tears burn in my eyes.

"You put it there!" I shout.

"Ms. Murphy," Ms. Southworth says. "Did you take Blake's wallet?"

"He put it there," I say, and point at Jason.

"I saw it in there," says the kid sitting next to me. "Her backpack was open and I saw it."

"Hey, wait. It's empty," Blake says.

"I think you had better give Blake back what you stole from him," Ms. Southworth says. "And then we had better go to the principal's office."

"I haven't got it. I didn't take it," I say.

"Give me back my tickets and money, man," Blake says.

"Ms. Murphy, if you do not give back what you took from Blake, Dr. Gorringe may have to call the police," Ms. Southworth says.

"I haven't got it," I say.

Southworth doesn't answer. She just takes me by the arm and marches me out of the class, down to Garbage's office.

Behind us, I hear Blake call, "Give her detention, man. Like, for a million years."

DETENTION

WHICH IS WHAT THEY DID. After Garbage went through my backpack, and threatened to have me strip-searched by Coach Stendahl if I didn't empty my pockets.

Strip-searched? Can they do that? I didn't know. I didn't want to find out. I emptied my pockets.

What they found was:

1. No lunch tickets
2. $1.37 in cash
3. All my private stuff.

I felt like a criminal. Which was really dumb, because I was the victim. And I was so mad I couldn't talk. Which made me cry again. Which made Garbage sure I was guilty.

"Well, Ms. Murphy, I'm pleased to see some contrition in you, at least," he said, while I stood in his office bawling like a baby. "It makes me feel relatively lenient toward you. If you confess, I'll be willing to let you off lightly."

And all of a sudden I get it. Garbage knows I didn't do this. And he's enjoying it.

When I can talk a little, I say, "Go to hell."

Garbage's face closes down like a steel door slamming shut.

"You will apologize at once," he says. "Or I will call the police. We have the evidence against you to expel you, and I will."

Like I ever want to see this place again. But the thought of the cops scares me. I don't know what would happen if he called them. Maybe they'd take me to Juvenile Hall. I've heard about that place.

"I'm sorry," I whisper.

"What? I didn't quite hear that," he says.

"I'm sorry." I try to shout it, but it comes out more as a squeak.

Garbage smiles.

"Very well. Now where are the money and the tickets?"

"I—don't—have—them. I—never—did," I say sort of one breath at a time. "It's—the—truth. A—Witch—Never—Lies."

Garbage sneers when I say that. Then sits there for a minute, thinking what he can do to me next. Finally, he says, "I'm sending a note home with you today, Ms. Murphy. You are to bring it back on Monday signed by your caregiver. If you do not, we will pursue this matter further. You are under detention for the rest of the afternoon. Go and sit in the lobby."

So I do.

There are three wooden chairs along the wall, the kind they call student desks, with a box under the seat and a wooden arm the size of a ping-pong paddle that is supposed to be the desk part. I take the one by the door.

A few minutes later, José Iturrigaray comes in. He looks around like he's afraid something's going to jump him. Then he sits down. He keeps one chair between us.

So where is Blake? If José's still got detention, he must, too. But he's a no-show.

I keep thinking how great a cigarette would be right now. But who needs a smoky aura? It is very difficult being a witch.

I don't know how long José and I sit there not looking at each other. It seems like a long time. Plus, I keep crying on and off. Some of it is because of how unfair everything is, and some of it is because I want that cigarette so bad. I hate wanting anything so bad. I hate having him see me cry. And I am out of anything to wipe my nose with.

Still looking straight ahead, José says, "I'm sorry."

"Huh?" I say.

"For asking if you was a witch. When that *pinche* Blake was there. I didn't see him around, or I wouldn't have done it. I'm sorry." He's still looking straight ahead.

"It's cool," I say, with my waterworks turning off. Then I ask, "What's a *pinche?*"

And José does something that is only slightly less weird than if he grew a second head, but weird in a good way. He blushes. I mean, he turns the color of raw gold.

"Never mind," he says. "It's dirty. I shouldn't have said it in front of you."

"Well, you did. So tell me what it means," I say.

"In English it don't—doesn't mean anything," he says. "It's so dirty you can't even think it in English. That's how dirty it is." And he slouches down real low.

"That's Blake," I say.

And then Blake comes though the door with his trophy in his hand and walks past us grinning like a rat with an extra piece of cheese and sticks his head in Garbage's office.

"Just wanted to say thanks again for letting me off detention, sir," he says loud enough to make sure we hear.

"You're welcome, Blake. Just let this be the start of a new era for you," Garbage's voice says.

Blake skips out past us and high-fives the air.

"You know any more Spanish words like *pinche?*" I ask José. He doesn't answer.

After a minute, I ask, "Why did you want to know if I'm a witch?"

He shrugs. "In Spanish there's two words. *Bruja,* that's a bad witch. And there's *curandera.* That's a good witch."

"That's neat," I say.

"My grandmother, she's a *curandera,*" José says. "So's my aunt. So that's why I asked. I wondered what kind you were."

I think it over.

"I'm both," I say.

"O ra le," José says.

"What does that mean?" I ask him.

He shrugs. "Check it out." He shrugs again. "I couldn't think of nothing else to say."

He takes out his notebook and starts to draw. I look over at what he's doing. It's this pyramid, only the stones look like they're moving, they're so alive on that paper. There's jungle in the background and a bird flying past, and that bird is just one line on the page, but it's all there, the wings, the body, and mainly the *flying.*

I watch while he builds that pyramid one line at a time, making the shadows on the steps, the little temple at the top, and huge, heavy clouds behind it all. I feel like I'm nearly there.

"You are truly cool with a pencil, José," I say.

He stops. "Wanna see some more?"

"Yeah!"

So he hands me his notebook. It's got homework in it. Stuff he started and didn't get finished. Words scrawled in broken sentences that wander off the lines. Diagrams all wrong. But all around them and over them are his pictures, and they are all so real and so right that they seem too big for the paper they're on. There's pictures of Aztec warriors, and one of the car I see him drive off in every day, and pictures of the guys in it, and it's like they can see me. And there's a couple of pages of a woman's face different ways, smiling, serious, holding a big spoon and tasting. One with her eyes closed, praying.

"Your mom?" I ask.

José nods.

"She's great," I say.

"I know," he says.

I hand his notebook back to him. "These are the best I ever saw," I say. "Thank you."

"It's okay," he says.

After a while, Garbage comes out. "You two may go," he says. He hands me an envelope. Sealed.

"Bring that back signed Monday or face the consequences."

José and I get up together without looking at him. He slouches out and I follow, trying to copy the way he walks, which I have realized is a very cool way.

SOME FLOW

THE SUN IS FARTHER DOWN than I thought it would be. I suddenly remember Laura. She is nowhere around, of course. I do not have her cell phone number or anything. She will probably think I ditched her. Damn. A Witch Never Lies, and now it looks like I did. But there's nothing I can do about it now. I can't even look her up in the phone book because I don't know her last name.

"We sat there a long time, man," I say to José.

José shrugs.

I see his ride waiting for him in a pool of tree shade. I think about how long those guys must have been waiting there. Whoever drives that car must love him a lot. It kind of makes me miss The Rentz for some reason. But I push that away. I have to.

"See you," I say.

José starts toward the car. I start for the street that runs in front of the school.

In front of the school, right along the street, there's this line of trees. Blake is standing under the one on the corner. He's got like three or four guys with him. There's also this pile of gravel where they're putting it down under the juniper bushes for landscaping. Blake and the other pigs are throwing pieces of it at something up in the tree.

I hear a yowl. A long up-and-down kitten voice that says, "For Goddess' sake, somebody help me before they kill me!"

I hear the pigs laugh.

Whatever cool I had left, I lose. My backpack hits the concrete by the flagpole. I start running.

"Blake, you *pinche!* You bunch of *pinches!*" I reach the gravel and start throwing it at them. These are big pieces, maybe two inches across.

Blake turns around and hits me with one of his. It thunks off my forehead.

"Open fire on Blondjoke," he hollers to the others.

Then Jose's voice says, "Don't call her Blondjoke."

SAY WHAT? I dreamed this, I think. *I remember it. But what happens now?*

Blake's ready with another piece of gravel, but he doesn't throw it.

"Hey, Blondjoke's got a boyfriend," he says.

José takes off his jacket like he's being cool, but he's mad. He's getting ready to fight Blake. Or all four of them.

"Get out of here," he tells them.

The cat yowls again. It's so high up in the tree I can't even see it.

"Go on, move it," José tells them, real quiet. He moves closer to Blake. So do I.

Blake laughs. Then he stops.

"Uh-oh," says one of the other little pigs.

"Uh-oh," says the second little pig.

I turn around. Coming toward us are José's guys, all three of them. They look like a wall, walking slowly together, side by side, all with their shades and mustaches like sword blades.

"Let's go," says the third little pig, and they turn and start running.

Blake gets about one step. Then I snake my leg out and trip him. I throw myself down on his back, making sure to land on my knees. I have great knees. Sharp as talons.

Then I let him up because José's guys are there.

For the first time, I see how different they are from each other. The tallest one has this great nose like a hawk. His sleeves are short and he's got a tattoo that says U.S. NAVY SEAL around an anchor and a lightning bolt. The second guy is a little shorter and has this great posture. He moves like a cat. A puma cat. Also, his torso is huge. He has scars on his arms where tattoos have been taken off. He's scary. The third guy is younger and thinner-looking, but not really thin. His muscles are just long and ropy. And they are all standing around Blake and me.

"Hey, man," says the tallest one. "What are you doing to that cat?"

Blake is getting up, looking around him. He is not happy.

"Don't touch me," he says. "Help, police!" He really does say it. Like some geeky lady in an old movie.

"Be cool, man," the tall one says.

"Police, police!" Blake hollers.

"He wants the police," the scary guy shrugs.

The tall guy reaches into his hip pocket. Blake gasps and cringes. I'll bet he thinks the guy has a knife.

What he's got is a badge.

"Sergeant Leon Iturrigaray, Jurupa PD," he says. "Now, let's talk."

Blake shuts up.

"José, introduce me," says Sergeant Leon Iturrigaray.

"This is Kestrel Murphy," José says. "And this *pi*—this is Blake Cump."

Leon waits. After a minute, José says, "And this is my brother Leon, and this is my cousin Victor—" the second guy, the fierce one with the posture "—and this is my other brother, Chris."

"Nice to meet you," says Chris.

"So *you're* Blake Cump," says Leon.

Victor doesn't say anything. He just looks at Blake and crosses his arms.

"Want to tell me why you did what you did to that cat?" Leon asks.

"It's not fair," Blake says. "I wasn't the only one doing it. I always get blamed."

The cat, which has never stopped yowling, climbs higher up the tree—I can hear it moving in the branches—and lets out an even bigger one.

"You know," says Leon, "I could start writing a bunch of tickets. Loitering. Cruelty to animals. Maybe even assault and battery—on both of you. But what good would it do?"

He puts a hand on Blake's shoulder. Blake's shoulder disappears under it. "Now, if I didn't know so much about you, if I hadn't heard so much about you and Miss Kestrel here from my brother, I might not feel the way I do about this. I might think that what I saw here today was all there is to know about you. Just a bunch of stupid kids. But every day when we pick him up, José tells us what happened in school that day. So I know there's more than that going on. So let's settle all this before it goes any further. Turn things in a new direction."

The water is deciding which way to flow. It flashes through my mind.

"So I want everybody to apologize and shake hands," Leon goes on. "José, you first."

José puts out his hand to me. I take it and say, "I'm sorry, José."

His head does this little jerk. "For what?'

"For thinking you were being a mean, creepy jerk when you were only asking me a question. You're really cool, man."

"I'm sorry, too," he says. He's blushing again, but not as bad as before.

"You didn't do anything," I say. "It was an accident."

José turns to Blake and holds out his hand. He doesn't say anything.

Blake turns to me and sticks his hand out.

"José's over there," I tell him.

"Oh, sorry. Didn't see you," he smirks, grabbing José's hand and pumping it up and down. "Awfully sorry, old man, for whatever I did. Pip-pip. Cheerio." He's using the fake English accent for some reason.

José doesn't say anything.

Blake takes my hand and says in his real voice, "And I'm really, really sorry I complained when you stole my wallet."

I keep my cool, which is just what he doesn't want.

"He's lying," José says. "She didn't take it. He had one of his friends put it in her backpack so she'd get detention, too."

"Whoa," says Leon. "Did you see this, José?"

"No, but I know. She sits right in front of Jason Horspool. He's like *that* with Blake." He holds up two fingers.

Leon rubs his mustache. He puts an arm around Blake. He says, "You know, Blake, you kind of remind me of me at your age. And that's why I'm not going to follow up on what my brother just told me about you. We're going to let it go. Because we're starting over, you and José and Kestrel and me. To go a different way. Because I think you really want to be a good person. Because almost everybody does, deep down. It's funny, but that's the way it is. So before you go, I'm going to tell you something somebody told me about how to be good. It was when I was in the Navy. My chief petty officer said to me, 'Iturrigaray, never write a check with your mouth that you can't cover with your ass.' It doesn't cover every moral choice you have to make. But it works for most of them. Remember those words, Blake."

I'm standing there tingling because those are the other words I dreamed.

Leon takes his arm off Blake. "I hope the next time we meet will be under more pleasant circumstances," he says.

Victor picks up Blake's trophy and turns it upside down. Ten pounds of pebbles fall out of it.

Blake takes it and goes.

"See you around," Leon calls after him.

SCRATCHES

"MAY WE TAKE YOU HOME?" Leon asks me.

"Thanks," I say.

We start to walk away. The cat hollers again.

"Wait," I say. "I can't leave him."

"He's pretty far up that tree," Chris says. "I don't think we can get him down."

"Give me a boost," I say.

José makes a stirrup with his hands and I'm up into the branches. When I stand up, the kitten is about four feet out of my reach. I ease myself up a little. The tree sways. Below me, the Iturrigarays spread out to break my fall in case I do. I go up another branch. The tree sways worse. The kitten looks down at me with huge, scared eyes. He hisses.

"Blesséd be," I whisper.

The kitten tries to back away. Then he realizes that he doesn't like going backwards uphill and turns around. I reach up for another branch, which shakes the one he's on just a little. He loses his grip and falls onto my face.

"RRROWWWOWWW," he says, and scratches me good. But my free hand grabs him and pulls him off.

"EEEYYYOWWWWWWWWOW," the kitten comments.

Now how am I going to get down? Especially with him scratching and twisting and trying to bite?

"Drop him," José calls up.

But I don't want to do that. Cats can get hurt that way. Everybody thinks they can't but they can.

"AAAAAOOOOOOOWWWOWWW."

"You better be grateful," I tell the kitten, and stuff him down my shirt. Then I get down as fast as I can, with the kitten trying to get out through the neck, the sleeve, through the waist, scratching me everywhere there is to scratch.

"Agh!" I holler, as he hooks onto my bra with his hind feet and pokes his head out beside mine. I stuff him back down, sit on the lowest branch of the tree, and jump. Then, on the ground, I reach up under my shirt and haul him out.

The cat is so little I could almost cover him with my hands. He's all gray except for a few white hairs on his neck. A really great gray, like a foggy night. But he's matted and kind of dirty. And he's totally skinny. He clamps himself onto my hand and starts biting like he's trying to kill it, which it feels like he probably will.

"What are you going to do with him?" José asks me.

"Maybe somebody around here owns him," Leon says. "But he looks pretty young to be given away. I think he's a dumper."

"I'm taking him home," I say. "Aunt Ariel will know what to do."

So we get in their car. The closer we get, the more beautiful I see it is. Besides the blue and chrome there are these delicate little black tracings all over it, like calligraphy. Some of it *is* calligraphy. On the fender it says Elena in long flowing swoops.

Chris gets in on the far side in the back. Leon and Victor

get in front. José holds the door open for me and I get in the middle in the backseat. And the seats are blue velvet, and the upholstery overhead is blue leather, and even the dome light has a blue bulb in it.

"This has got to be the greatest car anybody ever made," I say.

"Been in our family since 1960," Leon says. "Victor was born in it, on the way to the hospital."

"Who made it like this?" I ask.

"My father cherried it out the first time," Leon says. "After he died, it got pretty ratty. Chris fixed it up the second time."

He turns the key and the engine roars and we pull away from the curb. I feel like I'm riding home on a float, or maybe a carriage. I'm all scratched up, and the kitten hates that we're moving, but I just hold on to it, while my carriage takes me down the street.

When we get to Aunt Ariel's place, she's standing on the lawn.

José lets me out and stands there slouching again.

"When you didn't come home, I called the school," she says. "They said you'd been released from detention and they didn't know where you were."

I give her the note.

"I'm sorry," I say.

"Not as sorry as they're going to be," she says, stuffing the letter into her dress without reading it.

I think she means the Iturrigarays. "No, Aunt Ariel," I say. "These guys are cool. They saved me. José and his brothers and cousin all saved me and this cat from Blake Cump."

Ariel looks blank for a second. Then she gets it. "Oh, I see what you mean. No, dear, I meant the school, not these gentlemen."

"I'm Sergeant Leon Iturrigaray, Jurupa Police," Leon says. "I did a little intervention with the Cump boy and my kid brother this afternoon. Your niece, too. I hope everything's going to be a little calmer now."

"It's very nice to meet you, sergeant. I'm Ariel Murphy, Kestrel's aunt," Ariel says, shaking his hand. "And I hope you're right."

"This is José," I say, dragging him forward. "He does neat pictures. He's in my English class."

"How do you do, José?" Ariel says, offering her hand.

José takes it, gives it a little squeeze, ducks his head, and says, "'Lo."

"Listen, I gotta put this cat in the house before I bleed to death," I say. I run to the door, open it, and throw the cat inside. Then I run back.

"Would you like to come in, gentlemen?" Ariel asks.

"My cousin has to get to his dojo, and I have some errands to run before I go to work," Leon says. "Maybe we could take a rain check."

"I hope it rains soon," I say like a geek.

"I'll see what I can do," Ariel says out of the side of her mouth.

"Let my aunt see your car, okay?" I say. "José's brother did it."

José looks to Leon. Leon nods.

"Sure," says José.

So Aunt Ariel walks all around the car like she's studying it. I follow her. I notice that on the driver's side the beautiful lettering says Armando. She walks all around it and ends up in front of the grille.

"What's under the hood?" she asks.

"Basic Chevy juiced up to around three hundred hp," Leon says.

"May I see?" Ariel asks.

So Leon pops the hood and shows us this engine that could move a starship. Parts of it gleam silver and parts are painted red, and it's all clean. It's the cleanest engine I've ever seen. You could cook on this engine.

"*Que magnífico!*" Aunt Ariel breathes.

For the first time, Victor says something.

"You speak Spanish?"

"*Pues, un poquito,*" Ariel answers. "*He pasado varios tiempos en México estudiando con las curanderas. Pero no tengo la oportunidad usarlo mucho aquí. Desculpe.*"

Victor smiles. All his fierceness uncoils. "You sound good to me," he says. "For an Angla."

"She sounds better than you," Leon says, all serious.

"José speaks Spanish, too," I say, getting prouder of Ariel by the minute. "He taught me some today."

José ducks his head,

"*Y es usted el señor quien hizó este esplendor?*" Ariel asks Victor.

Victor grins. "No. The guy in the back did it."

Aunt Ariel walks around to Chris and says, "Beautiful work." Her voice is all soft.

"If you really like it, maybe you could come over to the shop sometime," he says, and his voice is all soft, too. "This is how I make my living. There's usually two or three street rods around the place at any one time. Other stuff, too. If you like cars."

"I will," says Aunt Ariel.

"We have got to get going," Leon says. "If Victor's any later, he'll have to fire himself." He drops the hood. It makes this great crumping sound. Then he slams his door. It's like he's putting on his armor. It *is* armor. It's all their armor, and the crest on their shield.

The Chevy takes off, low and slow and full of power and love.

I wave. *Blesséd be,* I thinksay.

FAMILIAR

WHEN WE GO INTO THE HOUSE, the kitten is nowhere. I start looking under furniture and in closets, but no way is he around.

Meanwhile, Aunt Ariel is reading the note from Garbage.

"Kestrel, would you come in here, please?"

I go in and sit across the kitchen table from her.

"What happened to you today?"

So I tell her. While I'm telling her, her face gets whiter and whiter.

"And did they search Blake and Jason, too?" she asks when I'm done.

"No," I tell her.

"That man is out of control, and he is not fit to be around children," Ariel says. Her voice is different. Man, is she mad. "He threatened you with something that would have been completely illegal if he'd actually done it. And I'm sure he knew that. I'd have sued the school district, and they'd have been glad to settle out of court. But they might keep him on afterwards. No, I'm going to have to find another way to change the flow." Her voice is smooth, but her eyes are blazing with witchfire.

Then, after a minute, she says, "But let's put this aside for now. We have a weekend ahead of us. Let's enjoy it."

She smiles at me, but she's still mad. I feel warm all over, thinking how fierce this aunt of mine is right now because of me. I almost feel sorry for Garbage.

But the kitten is still nowhere.

"Aunt Ariel, do you know a spell to bring a cat to you?" I ask.

She laughs and says, "There's one that works almost every time. Watch this."

She goes over to the refrigerator and opens it. She gets out some milk and pours it into a saucer. Then she slams the refrigerator door and calls "Here, kittykittykittykittykitty."

The kitten comes running into the kitchen from wherever he's been, mewing, and runs right over to the milk. He puts his face down to it and stands there, staring.

"He's too young to know how to drink," Ariel says. "Come here, Kestrel."

I go over and kneel down by the cat. He tries to run away, but I catch him and hold him.

"Put some milk on your fingers and let him lick it off," she says.

I do and he does.

"Now see if you can get him to follow your fingers down to the saucer," Ariel says.

After a couple of tries, he gets the idea. He drinks the saucer dry, hisses at us, and runs off again.

"We'll run an ad in the paper, but I suspect we have a cat," Ariel says.

"He'll be my familiar," I say.

Ariel shakes her head. "That's not something just any cat you find in the street can be," she says. "There are familiars with pedigrees going back centuries. We'll have to wait and see with this one. Maybe he has it, and maybe he hasn't."

"How will we know?" I ask.

"We'll know," Ariel says.

But I decide in my head that he's my familiar, no matter what. The universe knew getting a familiar is on my list. And now it's sent this cat. Maybe it's trying to make up for all the bad stuff that happened this week. Anyway, let Aunt Ariel run her ad. I'll chant a chant to make sure no one answers it. Help the flow along.

After dinner the phone rings. I wonder if it's Laura calling to bless me out for abandoning her, but it isn't. It's BD. He must be a little better if he can stand talking to me.

HERE IS WHAT WE SAID

BD: Hello, dear. How are you?
ME: Cool. How are you?
BD: Not so cool, but a little better, they tell me.

I don't say anything, so he goes on.

BD: What's school like?
ME: Well, there's this big building and they have classes and stuff.

Truth he can handle, right? But BD sighs this big long sigh. *His heart,* I remember.

BD: Have you got any friends yet?

I almost say, "Yeah. Her name's Ursula and she's got tattoos all the way up both arms and she's gonna get me into her gang," but I remember A Witch Never You-Know-Whats and tell him the truth I think he can handle.

ME: Not a friend, exactly. But there's this kid in my English class I like. He draws really neat pictures. We

hung out in detention today and his brothers gave
me a ride home in their lowrider, and Ariel asked
them in but they couldn't stay.

BD: What's his name?

ME: José Iturrigaray.

BD: Put my sister on, please. Now.

So Ariel gets on the phone.

AA: Yes, she did… Yes, I did… All right? Yes, they seem
like a charming family… Well, his brother is a police sergeant, but I don't think we ought to hold that
against him, do you? Ted, you're going to have to
stop worrying so much. You don't have that luxury
anymore. And you don't have cause. Kestrel is doing
very well. She's a delight to have around…. Yes, she's
not smoking. She's not smoking, her grades are
good, and she's starting to make friends. You should
be very proud of her…. Why don't you tell her
that?… It will mean more coming from you…it
would mean a lot…. Good.

She hands me back the phone.

BD: Honey, I just want to say that I'm proud of you.

ME: Thanks.

BD: Keep it up.

ME: Keep what up?

BD: Uh—everything you're doing.

ME: Okay, I promise.

Then we both hang there with four hundred miles of dead air
between us because he can't think of anything more to say to
me and I can't tell him any more truth and it sounds like even
what little I did tell was almost too much. And when I realize

that he's not talking because he hasn't got a clue about what to say, and that there's nothing I *can* say, and how much we do not compute, I want to cry. And I don't want him to hear that, so I hand the phone to Ariel and get out of the room.

> AA: No, she just left. I think you touched her very deeply, Ted. She's crying a little, I think…. Give yourself credit. You mean more to her than you know. You're her father, after all. No, I think she wants to be alone now. Take care. 'Bye."

THE END BUT NOT EXACTLY

Aunt Ariel puts down the phone and comes into the living room, where I'm balled up on the sofa with my knees in my eyes. She sits down and puts one of her great arms around me. I roll myself into her chest and we just hang on to each other for a while.

Finally, Aunt Ariel says, "He really does love you, honey. He just doesn't have a clue."

"How'd you know that's why I was crying?" I say.

"I'm a witch."

"Oh, yeah," I say. Of course she would know. "Will he ever get one?"

"It could happen. This heart attack could be the thing that breaks him open inside," Ariel says.

"Are there any spells we could cast that would help him?" I ask.

Aunt Ariel thinks. "A huge part of his problem is that he can't be who he was and he doesn't know who he can be instead."

I get this cold feeling. "You mean he might decide he doesn't want to be anybody?"

Ariel sighs. "It's possible. When someone comes to me for

a spell, at least they know what they want. That's a huge advantage. I guess the best thing we can do is ask the universe to show him who he wants to be next."

After that, she offers to take me out to a movie or down to the video store to rent whatever I want, but I turn her down. All I really want is to go into my room and write down what just happened.

When I am done doing that, I take one last look around for the kitten, but he's found someplace really great to hide. It's early, but I say goodnight to Aunt Ariel, close the door to my room and go to bed.

I sit there in the dark feeling my scratches and thinking about the day. I don't think I ever had one with so much good and bad in it. Blake was the pig of the world, but if he hadn't been, would I ever have found out how neat José is? Would I have gotten my kitten if it hadn't been for Blake? Would I have gotten to ride in that car? If Garbage hadn't sent that note home, would I have known how much Aunt Ariel loves me? I think about BD who can't compute me and now can't compute himself. But maybe now I can help.

Is the universe on my side or not? Ariel would say, "It's both." But that's not enough for me. The universe is in higher gear, and I want to know which way it's flowing.

I take a step back. I thinksay, *Interesting.* And it is interesting. But that's all I can tell.

I go over to the bed and pick up a pillow to throw it.

I hear this "Aaow." The kitten bounces up and dashes around the room. He was asleep under the pillow.

He hisses. He runs. He puts up a paw and scratches at the door.

I sit back down at my desk.

After a minute, he trots over to me. He pounces up on my knees.

I pick him up and hold him against my chest. He squirms,

then stops. He starts this tiny purr, like he's never done it before and isn't sure how it works. It gets stronger.

I try petting him again. First he scratches me again. But then I skritch him under his chin, and he stretches his jaw into my hand. His purr gets louder, so loud it shakes him.

It starts to flow into me. My familiar is trying to heal my heart. And it is working.

Interesting. Very interesting.

LAURA

THE NEXT MORNING, I NAME THE CAT. This is very important to keeping him. Ratchbaggit is what I call him. I don't know what it means, it just comes to me. It has a good, witchy sound.

Anyway, now I can cast the spell to make sure no one else gets him. I draw the sacred pentagram and put him in the middle of it. He gets up and runs away. I put him back; he runs. We do this about ten times.

Finally, I take my wastebasket and put it upside down over Ratchy and the pentagram. He hollers, and the wastebasket keeps making little jumps, but at least it holds him in place while I chant a spell of protection which comes to me from the same place I got the name.

Powers of darkness and powers of light
Don't let that ad come to sight
Of anyone who owned this cat.

I say this five times, once at each point of the pentagram, though I have to guess where they are because of the wastebasket. I think Ratchbaggit kind of likes it, because he calms down a little and the wastebasket jumps less.

Then I take the wastebasket off and let him run around. I write his name on a piece of special red paper with my special silver pen and light my black candle. I take another piece of paper and write Whatever Name He Was Before on it. I hold it over the flame. It crisps up, and his old identity is gone.

"Come on, Ratchy. Let's get some breakfast," I say.

He follows me into the kitchen, like any familiar would.

I give Ratchy some milk and me some cereal. It's good to sit there in the kitchen with the sun coming in through the windows and the quiet all around, just me and my cat.

When we're done, I decide to help the universe out by washing the dishes. I even dry them and put them away. While I'm doing this, the phone rings, and I get this flash: It's Laura.

"Oh, well," I say. Time to get my little ear blasted.

Of course it is Laura. Before she can talk, I say, "Listen, I'm sorry. They gave me detention yesterday. I didn't get home 'til practically night."

"Why did they give you detention?" Laura asks.

So I tell her and after five minutes it's like I'm talking to an old friend. And she's listening and going, "Uh-huh. Uh-huh. Oh, no," and, "Blake did *what?*" And I feel so good telling this to someone my own age that when I'm done, I don't want it to stop. So I say, "What's up with you?"

And for the next half hour we talk about everything. The Queens, how school sucks, and why chocolate is better than carob even though carob is sweeter.

Then Ariel comes into the room.

"Just a sec," I say to Laura.

"Listen, Kestrel," Ariel says. "I have to go to Costa Mesa this afternoon. I'm speaking to a group. Do you want to come along?"

No, I don't. But then I think, *Laura's interested in the Craft.* So I say, "Can I bring someone?"

"José?" Ariel asks.

"No, the girl who found my stuff—Laura," I say.

"Of course. If she wants to come, we'll pick her up in an hour and all have lunch someplace. How's that?"

Ariel looks even happier than I feel.

So I tell Laura, "Look, I've got to go to this thing my aunt's doing in Costa Mesa. Want to come along? We'll get lunch."

Laura practically squeaks, "Yes."

So we drive over and get her.

Her house is in a part of Jurupa I haven't seen before. It's the old part, with houses that are a hundred years old, some of them. There are houses like little castles and houses like Spanish missions and houses that don't look like anything but houses, but they are way interesting. The streets are quiet and the trees are friendly and make thick shadows on the pavement.

"These are nice," I say. I am very surprised to hear me say it.

"They are indeed," Aunt Ariel says. "Jurupa was the original Palm Springs. A hundred years ago, people used to come here to spend the whole winter, and get away from the snow. There are mansions on some of the hills that make these places look small."

"So what happened?" I say.

"Smog. People," Ariel says. "It stopped cooling off at night the way it did. The rich folks moved on and left their fantasies behind."

"So why do you stay here?" I ask. "It seems like you could live anywhere and do what you do."

Aunt Ariel doesn't answer at first. Then she says, "Spiritual ecology. There's something about this place that lies underneath the ordinary surfaces of things. And if you can touch it, it's very sweet and powerful."

Jurupa does not look like a place that has any ecology at all, let alone the spiritual kind. But I have to believe that Aunt Ariel knows what she's talking about. Or at least I have to believe that it's possible that she does.

But now we are in front of Laura's house. It is one of the Spanish-looking places. It is long and low and about twice as wide as Aunt Ariel's house.

When we ring the bell, there is a chime that sounds like a one-note song, and Laura opens the door.

"Hi," she says and smiles. "Thanks for coming."

Inside it's dark and cool and clean and makes me think of a library. There isn't even a television in the living room. But it feels peaceful.

Her rentz seem nice in a gray sort of way. They're pretty old to be rentz, but they turn out to be kind of cool. Their names are Arthur and Irene.

"How very nice to meet you," Arthur says, taking Ariel's hand. "I greatly enjoyed your last book. Your knowledge of folklore is most impressive."

"Thank you, Mr. Greenwood," says Ariel. "I've enjoyed all your books."

"You have?" Arthur says, like Aunt Ariel's just given him a present. "I'm surprised you've heard of me. So few people read poetry."

"Perhaps that's because so few poets write poems worth reading," Ariel says.

Arthur smiles.

So Laura's BD is a poet. I wonder how you get a job like that. Anyway, it's wicked cool that he and Aunt Ariel know about each other.

Irene says, "We're very pleased to meet you, Kestrel. How did you come by such a beautiful name?"

"Basically, I gave it to myself," I say.

"Wonderful," Arthur says. "More people should name themselves. It makes a great deal more sense than being named by a couple of strangers. Aztecs had five names, of increasing secrecy and potency. Very intelligent."

"Well, I like being named Laura," says Laura.

"Perhaps that's because we named you very carefully," Irene says. "We waited for four days, until we were certain you were a Laura."

"We might have waited longer, but the hospital wouldn't release you without a name," Arthur says. "Otherwise, you might still be known as 'Hey, You.'"

And he and Irene smile at Laura like she's made of gold, or maybe diamonds.

"We'd better leave if we're going to get lunch first," Ariel says.

"Yes, of course," Arthur says. "But I hope we can spend some time together soon."

"Perhaps you could come over for dinner," Irene says.

"That would be lovely," Ariel says.

And we're out the door and off to Costa Mesa.

Laura is just sitting in the back with me, smiling. Really quiet. I decide to try to loosen her up. I want more of the kind of talk we had on the phone.

"So how did your dad get to be a poet?"

"Oh, he just is, I guess," Laura says. "He teaches English at the community college, mostly."

"Every poet works at something else to make a living," Ariel says. "Arthur Greenwood has a national reputation."

"So your dad is famous?" I ask.

"Not really," Laura says.

"He would be, if poets became famous in this country," Aunt Ariel says.

After that, Laura stops being shy around Ariel and the three of us talk about everything under the moon until we get where we're going.

When we get to Costa Mesa there's this huge mall. We go to the food court and have lunch. Then we go up to the top floor and there's a bookstore called the White Goddess, and in the back of the store there's a big space with a garden fountain and plants in rock containers, and this audience sitting on cushions, waiting for my aunt.

They all clap for her, and Ariel lights a huge candle and says, "Merry met and blesséd be."

"Blesséd be and merry met," some of the people say.

Laura and I stand at the back and watch. I feel so proud that all these people are here, paying fifty bucks apiece, to hear my aunt.

Laura is leaning forward like she's afraid one of Ariel's words might fall on the floor before it gets to her ears. But a lot of what my aunt is talking about is stuff I already know.

After a while, I decide to look around the store.

"Want to check this place out?" I whisper to Laura. "I can teach you all this stuff later."

So she gets up and comes with me.

Besides books, the White Goddess sells crystals and DVDs and audiobooks and all kinds of supplies for the Craft. In the middle of the store is a big display of books Ariel has written. There are like six different titles. I didn't know she could do that! I'm so happy to be right here, right now, that I hug myself.

"This is so cool," I whisper to Laura. "My aunt is awesome."

"She's famous," Laura whispers back. "Didn't you know? She's been on television, and in *Personal* magazine."

Wow. I didn't know any of this. I guess that's how much BD and Aunt Ariel don't get along. I start thinking about how nice it would be to be part of a family like Laura's seems to be. I try to push the feelings away, but I can't. And—this is lame—I start to cry. Quietly. Just tears. No sobs.

Laura gets very quiet. Of course, she's pretty quiet anyway. But I appreciate it. She takes my hand, and I appreciate that. And then she hands me something to wipe my nose with, and I appreciate that even more.

After the lecture, Ariel signs about a thousand books and we drive home. Laura's full of questions for Ariel and the two of them talk all the way back to Jurupa. I just listen and think how the universe gets more and more complex the more you step back and say, *Interesting*…

When we get back to Laura's place, her rentz ask us in for a drink. Aunt Ariel has no problem with this. Neither do I.

We sit on a patio with a thatch of palm fronds over it. The furniture is all made of little branches and fits together like coral or the skeletons of little dragons. No two pieces are alike.

"Neat chairs," I say.

"My mother makes them," Laura says.

"These things are my wife's poems," Arthur says. "Unlike mine, each one is unique."

"Just bits of driftwood I find on trips," Irene says.

There's a little waterfall in the corner of the yard and its light is glittering on the brick wall beside it, and feathery jacaranda trees are catching the sun. It's so peaceful that when the clouds pass by, it's like they've come to visit, too.

Arthur disappears and comes back with a bottle and some glasses.

"May we have a glass?" Laura asks.

"I'm afraid not this time, dear," Arthur says. "It would be rude." Then he turns to Ariel and explains, "It's our custom to allow Laura one glass of wine with us. It's legal if one's parents give it to their child. But not under any other circumstances."

"Would you care for one, Kestrel?" Ariel asks me.

"Uh—sure," I say.

"Well, Arthur, I'll decline your kind offer since I'm driving. But if you give me a glass and I hand it to Kestrel, that will suit me, her, and the state of California. And then Laura can have hers."

The wine is chilled and a little sweet. It's my first glass of wine ever, and I try to notice everything about it, like the way it changes on my tongue after the first few sips. And here I am drinking it with a poet, and a mom who makes art furniture, and a girl who thinks I'm cool, and my Aunt Ariel.

Everyone talks a little, nobody talks too much, and everything that gets said seems to matter. I can't remember a conversation like this. Meanwhile, the jacarandas are dropping twigs and leaves and shadows on the lawn, saying, "Don't forget us. We're part of this, too," and the sun is blazing down the smoggy sky, but we're comfortable and cool under the palm thatch.

If *blesséd be* means anything, I guess this is what it means.

TAMALES AND COMETS

I DO NOT THINK THINGS can get any better. But then they do.

When we walk in the door of our place, Ratchbaggit runs out, sees us, hisses, runs away, remembers who we are, runs back, and tells me he's starving. I feed him the kitten food we picked up on the way home, and check the answering machine. No calls about a cat (of course), but there's one from Chris Iturrigaray.

Ariel calls him back.

"Yes, we'd love to come over tomorrow afternoon. About two? Good. See you."

She puts the phone down.

"What did he want?" I ask.

"To show me his shop," she says. "He's got a special car he's working on."

She's got this funny little smile on her face.

The next day we go over to Chris's shop. It turns out to be on this little street with only seven houses, two on each side, and three in a half circle where the street dead-ends. The shop is on the corner. It's just a house and a garage with a sign in the yard that says COCHES CLÁSICOS BY CHRIS. There are three cars lined up in the yard. The garage door is open, and there are all kinds of painting equipment inside.

I see José in there putting tape on the chrome of some little sports car.

"Hey, José," I holler.

He looks up, doesn't say anything, and goes into the house. A minute later, he's back with Chris.

We all walk around the car, which is little, and old, and pale cream.

"Good grief, it's a Cométe," Aunt Ariel says.

Chris and José look like they've just been electrocuted.

"Wow," says Chris. "When the guy brought it in, even I didn't know what it was."

"They only made eighty-five of them," Ariel says. "And only a few of those ever left France. Does it still have the Ford engine?"

"Oh, yeah," Chris says, and he's smiling like the sun coming up. "Nothing special about the engine."

"And they want it turned into a lowrider?" Ariel asks.

"Nah. Just cherried out," Chris says. "I don't just do lowriders. Everything on wheels needs paint."

So far, José still hasn't said anything.

"You help out here a lot?" I ask.

"Sometimes." He shrugs. Then he says, "How's the cat?"

I whisper, "Aunt Ariel put an ad in the paper for him, but no one's going to answer it. I've made him my familiar."

"What's that?" he asks.

"A special pet," I say. "Only witches get to have them."

"What's it do?" José wants to know.

"I'm not sure," I say. "I never had one before."

After that, José doesn't say anything. It's like Friday never happened or something.

Finally, I say, "You live around here?"

He points. "Down there. With my mom."

He means the last house on the street. It looks older than the others. It's Spanish-style, but a lot smaller than Laura's place. It's still cool, though. It's got white walls and a red tile roof and this little arch over the driveway.

"José," Chris says suddenly. "Take Kestrel home and introduce her. We'll be along in a few."

"Come on," José says.

He leads me down the street past yards full of kids who holler at us and wave.

"They all know you," I say.

"They're all my cousins," he says. "We own this street. Leon lives next to mom. Victor lives over there. My Aunt Carmela lives on the other side of us. There's a bunch of us, I guess." He shrugs. "My dad's dead. He was kind of old. I was an unexpected pleasure. That's what my mom says."

"My dad's almost dead," I say. "He had a bad heart attack."

"Mine, too," José says. "Is he getting better?"

"Yeah," I say. "Maybe."

I don't want to think about BD right now, or what it will feel like if he dies. I look back up the little street and think about all seven houses being filled with Iturrigarays. They all know each other. They all seem to like each other. They all seem to enjoy being Iturrigarays.

"It's like a castle," I say.

"Huh?" José says.

"This street. I don't know. It just seems like one," I say.

José looks back up the street, too. "You think it's like a castle?"

"Yeah," I say.

"Come on in," he says, and opens the door to his house.

Inside, there's about a hundred different women, all ages and sizes. The house is hot, with steam and great smells coming out of the kitchen, and everybody talking and there's that Mexican music with all the violins playing on an old stereo.

José kind of pushes his way into the kitchen and over to the stove.

"*Mami,* this is Kestrel," he says to this little old lady who's wiping her hands on her apron. "Kestrel, this is my mom, Mrs. Iturrigaray."

"Hi," I say.

"Welcome, Kestrel," she says. "It's nice to finally meet you. José talks about you so much."

He does?

But then I'm getting introduced around to all these aunts and cousins and nieces and no way can I keep everyone straight, and then Chris and Ariel come in and the whole thing starts all over again.

Then Leon comes in with his family, and Victor comes over with his girlfriend, and there's this little string of introductions. Victor looks happy. I don't think he's one-tenth as angry as he was the first time I saw him.

With Leon is this little old lady who looks like she must be about a hundred and fifty. She's about four feet tall and she walks like a mechanical doll. Leon says, "Ms. Murphy, Kestrel, I'd like to present my grandmother, Imelda Iturrigaray." Aunt Ariel kind of drops her eyes and says, *"Encantada, Doña Imelda."*

And the little old lady looks up into Ariel's face and says one word, *"Hermana,"* and there's this feeling in the room like Aunt Ariel's just been blessed.

Now that half the population of Southern California is in the living room, José's mother figures we have enough people to go outside. Everyone heads into the backyard and it's filled with tables—dining tables, card tables, boards on saw horses—all covered with different kinds of cloths and they're held down at the corners with little rocks in case a breeze comes up, and out comes the food.

Mostly, it's tamales. Gibungous mountains of tamales on every table. And to go with them there's salad and chips and salsa that makes your mouth explode, and cans of beer and soda in big tubs full of ice set in the shade along the house.

I sit next to José, of course, and Aunt Ariel sits at another table with Doña Imelda and Leon's family. I look around and I see that everyone's happy and talking and laughing, and Aunt Ariel and Doña Imelda have their heads together and it's like they're in some place of their own.

José hands me a cola and a paper plate full of tamales and I'm trying to think if I've ever had a better day in my life.

"You are so lucky," I say. "This is cool."

"You like this?" José says.

"Sure," I say.

"Good," he says.

We stay all afternoon. About sundown, the sea breeze finally finds its way to Jurupa and begins to blow the tablecloths around. The shadows start filling the yard and the tamales change flavor. Some of them are sweet and some of them are salty, and they don't have any meat in them. I figure they must be dessert, but then the dessert comes out and it's flan, which is caramel custard, in all different kinds of little bowls.

Then Doña Imelda leaves on Leon's arm and other people start to go. José and I help clean up, and the relatives take their tables and their dishes home, and the whole wonderful thing kind of vanishes like magick.

"Want to see my special place?" José asks me.

"Cool," I say.

It's the garage. It's real little and it's tucked in behind the house, not attached to it. It's so little that a modern car wouldn't fit in it. But it's got a red tile roof and white walls just like the house, and a door and a window. There's an old rug on the floor and a drafting table and one stool and a lightbulb hanging down and on the walls are José's drawings. A lot of them are on big sheets of paper.

On the drafting table there's a picture he's working on. It's of me. Actually, it's a bunch of pictures of me. There's me in a witch's hat, me with Ratchbaggit in my hands, and two or three others of my head turned different ways.

"Excuse me," says José, and tries to cover the picture up before I can see it.

"Wait, I want to look," I say.

"It's not finished yet."

"Can I look anyway?"

He shakes his head. "It's not finished."

"Come on, José," I say.

He stands there a minute, then takes away the piece of paper he was using to cover up the picture.

It's so weird to see a drawing of yourself. Especially by someone who can draw like José. It's not like a photograph. It's all these different ways of looking at yourself. At how somebody else is looking at you. It's a cool way of seeing, especially the way he drew my hands.

"You must spend a lot of time out here," I say.

"As much as I can," he says. "I like it a lot better than that *pinche* English class."

I turn around. "Why is English so much more *pinche* than any other class?" I ask.

"I don't get it," he says. "I can do the other stuff, but English—I get so nervous about that class I'm even afraid to go to school."

Then he blushes again, like he's told me more than he wanted to.

I remember those sentence diagrams mixed in with the drawings José showed me. How crippled the lines looked where he'd tried to take the words apart. And I get mad. Because nothing so simple should cause him so much trouble.

And, of course, one of my powers is grammar.

So I say, "Can you learn one thing a day?"

He looks at me like I'm dumb.

"Sure," he says.

"Well, there are forty-five grammar rules," I tell him. "And if you learn one a day you'll know them all in a month and a half. Besides, you already know some. I've seen your stuff, José."

He doesn't say anything.

"José, what's that thing called?" I say, pointing to his table.

"It's my drafting table," he says.

"And what's that thing over there?" I point at the window.

"The window."

"And that thing on the floor?"

"The rug."

"See, you already know what a noun is," I say.

"Huh?"

"Sure, they're just words for objects, that's all."

He thinks that one over. Then he says, "So that two-by-four up there is a noun. And the garage door. And the floor."

"Sure," I say.

"So what's the big deal?"

"There isn't one," I explain. "They just tell you there is so the teachers will have jobs."

José's thinking more.

"So what's a verb?" he asks.

"I'll tell you tomorrow," I say.

"Before English, okay?"

SWEET

WE GO LOOKING FOR AUNT ARIEL. José's mom tells us that she's over at Chris's place.

By now it's kind of purple and gray in the sky and lights are on in the houses. They're on in the garage where Chris paints cars. And that's where Aunt Ariel is. Kissing Chris. I mean *kissing*. She's practically bent backwards on top of that Cométe.

I stop in the middle of the street 'cause I don't want to interrupt anything, but mostly because I can't get my mind around it. Aunt Ariel? And Chris? On the first date? But this isn't even a date. We just came over and ate, and she started kissing.

I check them out. They look a little weird because she's about as tall as he is, but they look kind of cute, too.

"My aunt," I say. "Your brother."

"Yeah," José says.

It's cool, I say to myself. Then I say it to José.

And then I have this weird thought and it is so weird I think it must be for somebody else, but it is in my head. And it is this: I think about me and José kissing, just for a second. And then I am back to normal.

Then Chris and Aunt Ariel come up for air and she sees us and sort of waves.

"Come on over and see Chris's paintings," she says.

We finish walking across the street and go into the house. I see it's all a business. There are supplies and stuff stacked up everywhere, and a desk in one corner of the living room.

"I thought you lived here," I say to Chris.

"No, I live across the street with Victor," he says. "Just a couple of old bachelors."

We go into the big bedroom and instead of a bed there are pictures everywhere. Only not like José's pictures. These are paintings, big ones, on sheets of plywood. They're all kinds of bright colors and weird shapes, so big and strong they almost jump off the wood and start running around.

"This stuff is excellent," I say.

"The good ones are at the back," José says.

"May we see them?" Aunt Ariel asks.

José and Chris start dragging paintings out of a bedroom and setting them up around the house. By the time they're done, it looks like José's special place, in color. Aunt Ariel and I walk around looking at them.

"Where do you get your ideas?" I ask.

"Just stuff I see around the neighborhood, mostly," says Chris.

Around the neighborhood? On what planet?

"This one's the sun coming up in my mother's kitchen," he says, looking at something all black and orange with red spots hiding in it.

After he says that, I can see it. The tree in her backyard would look like that if you saw it from all angles at once instead of just the side by the window. The long straight lines must be the shadows, and the orange and red are the sun. Well, duh. I should have seen that myself.

And they're all like that. Once Chris tells you what it's a

picture of, you can see it. What a neat way to do painting. If these things were spells, I bet they'd work every time.

Aunt Ariel is walking around really quiet, taking everything in. Finally, she says, "Have you ever had a show?"

"Those are tough to get." Chris laughs.

"There's a woman in my coven who's part-owner of a gallery in West L.A.," Ariel says. "I think she ought to see these. Would that be all right?"

"Anytime a friend of yours comes it will be all right," Chris says.

Then Ariel decides it's time to go home, and I have to admit Ratchbaggit has been alone a long time. So we say goodbye to José's mom and everyone else, and Chris and José walk us out to our car.

Chris and Ariel give each other another kiss. It's not as long as the last one, but it's no see-you-arounder. Then we get into the car and drive home.

"This was maybe the best day of my life so far," I say as we turn the corner. "Except maybe for yesterday. I can't make up my mind."

"Doña Imelda," Aunt Ariel says. "I used to hear about her from other *curanderas* when I went to Mexico. They all knew about her, but nobody knew where she was. Once I met an old woman who claimed to have known her when they were both young. She said she thought Doña Imelda had gone to the United States, but she didn't know when or where. And here she is. Right in Jurupa."

I wonder if this is that spiritual ecology thing Aunt Ariel was talking about, or if it is just the universe messing around.

"What was that thing she called you?" I ask.

"*Hermana*. Sister," Aunt Ariel says. "And you know what else?"

"What?"

"This party we were at today. It's called a *tamalada*. Tamales are the most labor-intensive food in Mexico. They're so hard the women make a party out of making them. The work those women went to. And then they invited us." She reaches over and puts her hand on mine. "Kestrel, if it hadn't been for you, none of today would have happened."

"*Chris* would not have happened," I say.

"Chris has most definitely happened," Ariel says.

"Like a comet," I say, being a brat. "Oops, I mean a Cométe."

But Ariel says, "Well put," with this funny smile.

Then I say, "Did you cast any spells to make sure we had a good time?"

"Kestrel," Aunt Ariel says. "When you've been in the Craft awhile longer, you'll begin to see that a huge part of magick is perception. Like Chris's paintings. He takes what he sees and turns it into magick."

"But that sounds like you're saying magick isn't true," I say.

"No. No. No. What I'm saying is, you have to learn to see the magick first. Then you can work with it. Going at it the other way, and trying to force life into some pattern you've decided you want is the long way around. And very uncertain."

I know she's talking about me, and it makes me mad, a little. But I take a step back. I try to see the magick happening. It did happen, all these last two days. I didn't make it happen, but I was part of it. José didn't start it. Neither did Laura or Aunt Ariel. But we're all tied up together in it, and it's flowing with us and around us and—

I start laughing. I keep laughing, and I laugh so hard I bend over.

"What's so funny?" Ariel asks, but I can't answer. Finally I straighten up and say, "You want to know who made this day happen? You want to know who made everything happen? Blake and the Queens!"

We pull into the driveway where the black garage door with one white dot shines in our headlights.

I get out of the car, wave my arms over my head and shout, "Thank you, Queens! Thank you, Blake Cump! I just had the best two days of my life! You *pinches!*"

MONKEY BAR WORDS

MONDAY COMES. Garbage calls me into his office. I hand him back his note. And another one Aunt Ariel wrote this morning. He reads it. His face gets as white as hers did on Friday.

Then he says, "I think it will be best for all concerned if you are moved to Mr. Hall's sixth-period English class to separate you from Blake Cump."

"Cool," I say. Mr. Hall is a great teacher. I will still help José with his grammar after school or at lunch. That will mean more time with him, and that's cool, too.

And that's it. Garbage looks down at his desk and doesn't say anything.

I head for the door. "The universe is gonna get you," I say quietly as I leave.

He doesn't look up.

I see Blake Cump. He grins at me like he's got this big secret, but he moves away from me when I come down the hall.

"Hey, Blake, thanks! Things went great," I say.

He smirks. But he also turns so his back is to the wall. Like maybe he's just a little scared.

Gotcha.

I see José later, and at lunchtime we meet by the monkey bars…which Richard Milhous Nixon Union High School has because it used to be Richard Milhous Nixon Elementary School.

"Hey, José, I'm starting a coven. You in?" I say.

"I don't know. What is it?" he asks.

"It's a witches' club," I say.

"Do you got to be a witch?" he says.

"Well, duh. Of course," I say.

"Well, duh, I'm not a witch," he says.

"Okay, you don't have to be a witch to join my coven," I say. "See, I've decided I'm not a regular witch. I'm a special kind. I do majix. M-A-J-I-X. It's different from regular magick. It's all about developing your own powers. So we have our own rules about covens, and you don't have to be a witch. You just have to develop your own powers."

"Are we good or bad?" José asks.

"Both," I say. "'Cause that's what we already are."

José nods.

"But what if I don't have any powers?" he says.

"You do. Everyone does. Just not everybody knows what they are. In fact, most people go their whole lives without finding out what they are. But we don't."

"I don't know," José says. "I mean, I want to be in it. But what if I can't figure out what my powers are?"

"I know what one of them is already," I say.

"What?" José asks.

"Drawing," I say. "The way you draw is almost a majix. I'll bet you could turn it into one if you tried."

"Like how?"

"Well, you could try drawing pictures of things you wish for," I say. "Then I could put them in my pentagram and say chants for them. Then we'd step back, think, *Interesting,* and see what happened. If you got what you wanted, we'd know that worked. If something else happened, we'd know that."

"Okay. But suppose I draw something like Blake getting kid-napped and eaten by aliens and it happens," José says. "Could I get arrested?"

"No," I say. "Because we'll burn the pictures as part of the ceremony."

"No way are you burning my pictures," he says.

"Okay, forget it," I say. "We'll only burn one if it happens. Destroy the evidence."

José thinks it over and says, "I'm in."

"By the way," I say. "Garbage is throwing me out of English. To keep me and Blake apart."

José hunches up. "You still gonna help me?"

"Every day," I say. "Until you know every *pinche* rule."

He just stands there.

"Hey, José," I say. "What's a noun?"

"Monkey bars," he says. He doesn't sound happy.

But I see the monkey bars are the perfect way to teach our next lesson.

"Well, I guess I'll *climb* up," I say, and I do.

"That's for little kids," says José looking up at me.

"*Come* on," I say. "*Join* me."

"I don't want to," he says.

"Maybe I'll *swing* back and forth," I say. "Or *hang* upside down."

José looks at me like he's disgusted. Then he gets it.

"I *don't want* to," he says again.

"Why *don't* you *want* to?" I say.

"Because I *don't feel* like it," he says. "Because it *looks* stupid."

"No it *doesn't*," I laugh.

"Yes, it *does*. It *makes* you *look* like a kindergartner."

"Man, José, you *are* so smart," I say.

He climbs up beside me.

"Verbs are just monkey bar words," he says. "Why didn't they say so?"

We walk around for a while, just talking and saying the verbs extra hard. By the time the bell rings, José is forgetting to slouch.

COVEN!

GYM IS VERY BUSY. I don't even get a chance to thank T&A for my great weekend. No chance to talk to Laura about the coven, either. So I text her, and she calls me back.

"I'd love to join," she says. "But there's something I need to tell you that may make you change your mind about asking me."

"Shoot," I say.

"It's my parents," Laura says. "They talked about you and your aunt a lot after you left. They said it was the best time they'd had in months. But they don't believe in witchcraft or anything like that."

"Laura, A, your rentz are cool," I say. "B, mine don't believe in it, either. C, at least yours are polite about it. So, D, come on over to my place after school on Friday and we'll get started. Okay?"

"Okay," Laura says, all happy.

I open this book to where it says Things to Work On and put a check mark beside Start My Own Coven.

There is one more thing on my to-do list for today.

No one has called about Ratchbaggit and it has been three days. So it is time to let him go out and explore.

First, I put him on the pentagram and put the trash can upside down on him. I say a chant I have been thinking up. It goes:

Powers of darkness and powers of light,
Keep Ratchy safe by day and night.

After I've said it at the five points of the pentagram, I take him to the back door and let him out.

He goes hopping across the grass, and my heart hops, too. This is hard, letting him go, wondering if he's going to come back. But I have to do it. If he's really my familiar, he'll return to me. If he doesn't, I'll be worried sick.

Aunt Ariel is out with some of her coven and won't be home 'til late. So I just hang out, doing my homework without being able to concentrate on it, watching a movie, reading. And every minute I'm thinking about Ratchy.

The sun goes down and he doesn't come.

I call, "Kittykittykitty," and he doesn't come.

I call it again every hour until I go to bed, and he doesn't come.

Aunt Ariel comes home. I tell her Ratchy's out. Of course she says, "Blesséd be."

Then we go to bed.

And just after I get under the covers, there's this thump against the window, and when I open it, there he is hanging on the screen and yowing like he's saying, "Where have YOU been?"

I unhook the screen and lift him off it. He starts purring as soon as I touch him. Two minutes later, he is asleep right in the middle of the bed.

MAJIX

I get up, write this, and put a check mark next to Get a
Familiar on my to-do list.

The rest of the week is very ordinary. My new English class
puts me in with Laura, and Tiffany of T&A. My seat puts me
in a good spot to keep an eye on her. But nothing happens. I
figure the spell Ariel and I cast must have given the universe a
shove in the right direction.

José and Laura and I spend lunch planning what we're going
to do Friday, and when the day comes, we're ready.

Aunt Ariel has offered the garage for our meetings, but I turn
her down. A coven should have its own place, and I have
picked out ours. Under this big sycamore tree in the backyard.

For an altar we have a table Laura's mom made that she said
we could have. It has legs like a giant spider, which is perfect.
José's mom dyes a bedsheet black for us, so we have a cloth for
it. Aunt Ariel takes me to one of those science stores where
they sell telescopes and stuff, and I buy that kind of mobile with
all the planets hanging down. This will go over the altar on
Friday and we will be ready.

Meanwhile, I have been working out the majix we're going
to do. We are all bringing three things for the altar: something
we're proud of, something we're afraid of, and something we
want to work on.

The sun is bright and it's hot enough to fry asphalt that afternoon. I kind of wish we could have done this at night, but
it's cooler under the tree, and anyway when is it too hot to
invoke the universe?

We spread out the black cloth, and on it I put: this book, a
mirror, a wand made of oak, a brass plate Ariel loans me, some
sage, and a statuette of the Goddess I brought with me from
my old altar. Her arms are raised, and she's holding the moon
in her hands and on her stomach is a spiral.

"Okay," I say. "Now the first thing we're going to do is cast
a circle. You can't do anything else until you've done that."

I light the sage and do the circle-casting thing, with José and

Laura following me around and saying what I tell them to say. They mumble, because although we've been working together since Monday, they're still shy with each other. This is cool. The universe gets shyness. I figure it's why there are so many corners and shadows.

When the smoke has waved around the altar like fairies' hair and the smell is mixing with the faint mintiness of the sycamore leaves, we are ready.

"Okay," I say. "Now we can place our three things on the altar. I guess I'll start. First, here's the thing I fear."

I lay down a photograph of BD.

"It's my dad," I say. "He's had a heart attack and I'm afraid he won't get better. Who's next?"

José lays down his English book.

"Here's what I'm afraid of," Laura says. "I found it in my backpack today."

It's a scrap of notebook paper. It says: WERE GOING 2 GET U.

"Just put it on the altar," I say.

Laura lays it down.

I pick up the mirror.

"I made up this spell this week," I say. I hold the mirror over the picture of BD and say, "May this mirror take all my fear and change it to its opposite. Now you guys say, 'Blesséd be.'"

They do.

I hand the mirror to José.

"I can't say what you said," he says. "I don't talk like that."

"Say it your own way," I say. "Remember, this is majix."

"I hope this mirror takes all the bad stuff about English and turns it to good stuff so I don't have to take English anymore," José says. "Is that right?"

"Blesséd be," I say, and Laura says it after me.

I hand her the mirror.

She holds it over the note.

"May this mirror take all my fear and turn it to its opposite," she says. "Blesséd be."

"Blesséd be," José and I say.

"Now, what we're proud of," I say. I lean on the altar, spreading my arms wide enough to grab the ends. "I'm proud of this."

"Me, too," says José. "But I brought this."

He lays an English paper on top of his book. It has a B on it and the words *Big Improvement* on it at the top.

"José, man, you *rock*," I say.

"Whatever," he says, and blushes.

Laura lays down a copy of one of Ariel's books.

"I'm proud to know your aunt," she says. "I'm proud to be your friend."

Which makes me blush, I think. But anyway, I hold the mirror up to the sky and angle it so José and Laura can see the smoggy blue reflection.

"As we have received blessings, so we offer them up," I say. "Say *Blesséd be.*"

And they do.

"Now what we want to work on," I say.

I pick up the wand and touch the grimoire.

"I will this book to be the best it can be, and I ask the universe to help me," I say.

And José and Laura say, "Blesséd be," without needing to be told.

José lays some of his pictures on the altar and takes the wand.

"I will my drawings to be the best they can be, and I ask the universe to help me."

"Blesséd be," Laura and I say.

Laura takes out a little statuette of a ballerina. She's wearing a dress of real cloth. She's not pretty, but she's strong, and she's got one foot pushed forward like she's saying, "Here I am. Don't try to pretend I'm not."

Laura says, "I will myself to be as brave as I can be, and I ask the universe to help me."

José gives her the wand and she touches the statue.

We say, "Blesséd be."

"Okay," I say. "Now we all take time to open ourselves to the universe and each other and think how we can use our powers to help the others in the coven. Remember, it has to be using your powers."

I hold out my hands, and José, Laura, and I link up over the altar.

"Close your eyes," I say.

We stand there under the sycamore tree and I can feel the breeze start to blow. It rustles the leaves and the little paper planets over our heads make soft little *tok-tok* sounds as they hit together.

Something wants to talk to us, I thinksay. *May we be open to hear it. Blesséd be.*

The wind stops and the *tok-tok* sounds are quiet. But I know we have been answered. I just don't know what the answer was.

When I think about five minutes have gone by, I open my eyes.

"Okay," I say. "What have you got?"

"Nothing," says José.

"I don't even know what my powers are," Laura says.

"Okay, okay," I say. "This week I'll use my imaging powers to start you guys developing yours. Just be open, okay? If it works, things'll start coming to you."

"I'd rather you worked on the Queens," Laura says.

"I'll do that," José says. "I'll draw something."

"What?" I want to know.

"I don't know." José shrugs. "I never tried to draw something not happening before. But don't worry. I'll figure something out."

"Thank you," Laura says, and smiles.

"Next Friday good with everybody?" I say.

It is. So we uncast the circle and strip the altar.

It is then that we notice José's essay is missing.

Laura's note is gone, too, but we find that in the corner of the yard. José's essay is nowhere.

"The wind must have blown it," José says. "Damn. I wanted to keep that."

"No," I say. "This is cool, José. I think it means the universe is telling you it's taken your problem and started solving it. It kept Laura's note here with us to work on 'cause it's not over yet."

"Makes sense." José shrugs.

"Makes too much sense for me," Laura says.

And that's how we end. I'm worried about Laura. But I think I'm going to like being head of a coven. Explaining things to my friends feels good, especially when I didn't know I knew all that a second before I said it.

Maybe I got it from the wind.

HERO

THE NEXT MONDAY AFTER SCHOOL, I see José with Laura. He takes her over to the *coche*. Leon gets out. He's wearing his cop uniform for the first time since I have known him. He looks more like a police general than a sergeant. If they have generals in the police.

José introduces them, and the three of them walk around together, while half the school watches and pretends they're not.

I take a step back. Interesting.

T&A and the rest of the Queens are holding court at the side of the building. They don't stop talking, or act like they've seen Leon, but the guys with them never take their eyes off him.

He waves at me. I smile and wave back. Then, a few minutes later, the *coche* takes off with Leon and José. I go over to Laura.

"What's up?" I say.

"Majix," she says. "Look."

She takes her binder out of her backpack and shows me a

picture José has drawn tucked into the front. It is Leon standing next to Laura with his arm across her shoulders.

"José was making this for me yesterday and his brother saw him doing it. So he asked who the girl was, and José told him all about the Queens. So Leon said maybe he should come by and make the picture for real."

Her eyes are shining.

"Way to go, universe," I say.

José gets it.

Aunt Ariel is also getting it. From Chris. I hardly saw her this weekend. In fact, Saturday night, I waited up for her to come home. Which she did, after I had fallen asleep in the chair in the living room.

"Oh, Kestrel dear, that is so sweet," she said when she woke me. "No one ever waited up for me before. Were you worried?"

"No," I said. "I'm not some little kid waiting for Mommy and Daddy to come home. I just wanted to know how it went."

"Good," she says, so sweetly that I know she doesn't believe me, and we go to bed.

The next day, she says, "You know, Kestrel. I think I'm going to have to break down and sign up for a cell phone plan. I've always been smug about not needing one. But now, with us living together, I think I do. Just so we can keep in touch."

"Whatever," I say. Because I am not worried when she stays out half the night. Not really.

But she does get one, and now my little silver-and-black cell that does everything except fly and make ice cream starts buzzing. Ariel calls to check in when she's out with Chris. José calls to talk about what to draw, and about Ratchy. Laura calls to talk, even though we just did at school. Plus texting.

And my cell phone is part of how I become a hero this Thursday.

It is after school. Aunt Ariel is working on *Grimoire*. Ratchy is out being fierce. José is busy, and Laura has some kind of class she just started.

Also, I have gotten something from The Rentz today. It is my bike and helmet and stuff, which they have kindly sent me.

My bike.

I mean, I'm glad to see it again. It's a good one, and kind of a friend. But getting it means something. Somethings. It means, "We want you to have this because you probably need it and we know you love it." But maybe it also means, "You aren't coming back for a loooong time." And there isn't a letter with it, or a note, or anything. I mean, how hard would that have been?

So I just sit in the front yard with it for a while, trying to decide how I feel. Which I can't.

Anyway, I decide to get on it. Just to ride around the hood. Which is not much but houses and a little strip mall down the street.

So I go there first, and I buy a bag of chips, just so I had some reason to come down this way in the first place. But I do not want the chips. I don't want anything I can buy. I want someplace to go that is not just back to Ariel's house.

The only place I can think of is school. Don't ask me why. Ask the universe.

So I toss the chips in the trash, and pump up there.

When I get there it is about four thirty. The flag is down. The parking lot is empty. Someone has put I AM NOT A CROOK all over the base of the bust of Richard Milhous Nixon's head and then crossed out the NOT.

It is quiet. The loudest thing is the sound of the chain on the flagpole slapping against the pole itself, sad and tired.

I chain my bike up and start walking around.

There is something about being at a school when you don't have to be there. It makes you feel better, because you can leave anytime you want to.

Anyway, I start walking around the outside of the buildings.

Why am I doing this dumb thing? Because I can't think of anything else to do right now. The wind is blowing softly across the grounds and the trees are filled with the voices of the ghosts of old students who can't think of anywhere else to be, either. But at least I am here on my own time.

"Hey, losers," I say, and wave to them.

But while I'm doing it, I hear this kind of WHUMP! and a voice hollers, "Oh, shit!" and I smell gasoline and see this big hand of flame and smoke reach up from the far end of the building.

I whip out my cell. I start taking pictures. Then, I start to dial 911. Then I don't.

You know how in schools they always have those fire extinguishers behind glass doors? You never saw anyone actually break one in your life, but you always hoped you'd get to be the one to do it, even if it meant saving your school from burning down? You know how they have those alarms, and it's illegal to break the glass and pull one down unless there really is a fire? Well, I broke the glass and I pulled the alarm. And by the time the fire engines showed up, there I was spraying foam on the place where somebody had tried to torch the building.

These two big trucks come roaring across the campus with their sirens and lights and they get the hoses going and the thing is out in a few minutes.

That whole side of the school is a huge, gross black-and-gray mess. The water is still running off it, and the stinky smoke is hanging over the school and the houses around it.

The fire guys in their yellow coats and their helmets come and stand around me and say things like, "Are you all right?" and "Good going, girl" and "Look at that wall. We'd have lost this whole wing if she hadn't been here."

All of which makes me feel very cool. But then it gets even more interesting.

Because this detective comes and starts asking me questions like, "Did you see who started the fire?"

I have been waiting for someone to ask me this. I nod and pull out my cell and show him the guy running away with the gas can in his hand. It's just a few seconds, and you can't see his face, but the cop is pretty excited.

"Did you see where he went?" he asks me.

"Sure," I say. "Come with me."

I lead him over to the Dumpsters.

"In there," I say.

So the detective takes a step back. He puts his hand inside his jacket.

"Are you sure someone's in there?" he says.

I do not answer him. I just take the Dumpster lid and throw it back so it crashes good and hard against the back.

Out comes the detective's gun. He says, "Come out of there. This is the Jurupa Police."

Something that sounds like a huge rat scuttles around inside, but nothing comes out.

"Come out now," says the cop.

By now there are more cops, three of them. And they've got the Dumpster surrounded. More are coming. I hear the sirens.

Now there are five cops, and one of them is Leon.

He walks over to the Dumpster, looks down into it. Then he swears. He reaches in with one of his derrick-sized arms and up comes Blake Cump, twisting and crying.

"I didn't do it. They made me do it. I always get blamed." Then he sees me. "She did it. She made me do it. I almost got killed."

Blake's shirt is singed and he smells like a filling station.

22

BLAKE

IN CASE YOU'RE WONDERING one hundred years from now: No. Garbage Gorringe does not make me Orthogonian of the Week. He's not going to do that for somebody who doesn't wear the sucky uniform just because she saves his sucky school.

This is cool, because I do not want to be Orthogonian of Any Week, but he still should have done it.

I am in the paper, though:

GIRL, FOURTEEN, SAVES SCHOOL FROM ARSON

Susan Murphy, who prefers being called Kestrel and claims to be a witch, gives the universe credit for her being in the right place at the right time to save Richard Milhous Nixon Union High School from the firebomb of an arsonist Thursday.

"I just rode my bike up that way," she said. "I don't know why I went there. I never hang out at school after the bell rings."

(Actually what I said was "I never hang out at that sucky-hole loser academy one minute longer than they make me." So much for truth in newspapers.)

Anyway, it goes on to tell you exactly what you already know, except for Blake's name, on account of him being too young and "innocent" to have his name in the paper just because he tried to torch the school. I will not quote you the rest of it because you already know more about what really happened than they put in the paper. And also because what happens next is way more interesting.

Today is Saturday. José calls me up and says, "I got to talk to you."

The way he says it, I know he's scared.

"So talk," I say.

"I can't just talk," he says. "I have to show you something."

So I bike over there and meet José in his special place.

He unfolds a piece of notebook paper.

"I just started doing it," he says.

The picture is not finished. But it shows Richard Milhous Nixon Union High from the front and flames are coming up behind it.

Oh, man, it worked. First Laura and now this. José has majix to the max. No wonder he's scared.

"It's cool," I say. "The fire's out. Blake's in trouble. You're developing your powers, that's all. Great developing, by the way."

"But did I make Blake do it?" José asks.

That's something I hadn't thought of.

"No," I say. "Because you didn't put Blake in the picture."

"But the picture's not finished," he says. "Maybe I was going to put Blake in."

"Maybe we'd better ask Ariel," I decide after a minute.

"No way, man," José says. "Nobody else can know about this."

But Ariel has to know. Because we have to know what's going on. And we had better ask fast, before she and Chris take off for the evening. I make José see this, and we head back to our place.

José tells her the story, with me helping. She looks at the picture.

Then she looks at us over the tops of her glasses and says, "So your question is, are you responsible for what Blake did?"

"Yeah. Kind of," José says.

"Good one," Ariel says, and pulls her nose. "Suppose I say no. How does that make you feel?"

"I'm not sure," José says.

"Better or worse?" Ariel asks.

"Well, relieved. But it doesn't seem true, exactly," José says.

"Then suppose I say you are responsible?" Ariel says.

"I get mad," José says. "It's not fair to blame me for what he did."

Ariel nods. "Then suppose I say that you may be partly responsible?"

"What do we do if I am?" José asks.

"If *we* are," I say. "I gave you the idea."

"I'm glad to hear you say that, honey," Ariel says to me. "You're both realizing something important about the Craft. About any power, really. When you take it on, you acquire a certain responsibility with it. And in this case, you don't really know how much responsibility, or what kind. But you do feel there's some, or we wouldn't be having this talk."

"So what do we do now?" José asks.

"Take appropriate responsibility," Ariel says.

"But what kind? How?" I say.

"I have an idea," Ariel says. "Actually, it's just the beginning of an idea. But maybe Leon and Victor can help me turn it into something. Have you got Leon's number at work?"

So Ariel calls Leon and Leon calls back. They talk about Victor and then she calls him.

The next few days it's Ariel-and-Leon-and-Victor-and-

Laura's-mom, who it turns out is a psychiatrist-when-she-isn't-making-tables kind of woman, and it's all about Blake.

One of the biggest parts is what happens with Laura's mom. Because she talks with Blake, or hypnotizes him or something, and decides that he doesn't have the profile of a real arsonist. (Of course not. He has the profile of a perverted rat, with bad teeth.)

But Ms. Greenwood's opinion is like huge, apparently. Because Blake does not even get expelled or anything. Instead, she and Aunt Ariel come up with something that persuades me that my aunt is really off her broomstick.

Because what they all do is go to the court and talk it around with some judge and get Blake into his own personal diversion program. With Victor.

The deal is, Blake shows up at school at 2:30 p.m., from which he has been expelled, and gets into the *coche*. He rides down to Victor's dojo. And he works there until it closes. And he gets karate lessons for pay. And being expelled doesn't do him any good because there's this home teacher who gives him stuff to do and if it isn't done, he answers to Leon and Victor.

All this is Ariel's idea. And today is the day it began.

When I found out, I told José, "He'll never do it. Not in a million years."

"He's agreed," José says. "He's figured out some really bad stuff could happen to him if he doesn't."

"He's lying. He always lies."

"Maybe," says José. "But there are some guys in this world it's very bad to lie to. Leon and Victor are at the top of the list."

Which was true, so I had to be there to see Blake get killed.

So today after school we all ride down to Victor's dojo in the *coche*. It was Leon and Victor in the front seat, José and Chris in the back, with Blake between them, and little me in the cargo space behind.

Blake had been there right on time, looking scared, but trying not to show it.

"So are we gonna break bricks with our hands today?" he asks as he gets in.

Victor doesn't say anything. Leon starts the *coche* up and we head downtown.

"When do I get my black belt?" Blake says.

"Belts are to hold up pants with," Victor says. "Karate is not about belts, or taking people out with your feet, or anything that you think it is. And you won't learn any of that stuff until you show me you've learned a lot of other things first."

"Bogus," says Blake.

Victor says nothing. Real loud.

We get to the dojo. It is the first time I have ever been there. It is in a strip mall with a big sign over the door that says NUEVO MUNDO DOJO in graceful black letters that look kind of Japanese.

"Great sign," I say. "Did you do it, Chris?"

"Nope," Chris says. "José."

And José ducks his head in that way he does when he's feeling shy, that way I like so much.

"Come in for a minute," Victor says.

The dojo is simple and right, which makes it beautiful. I can almost taste the quiet. The walls are white and the floor is blue. It's covered with blue mats. In one corner is what looks like a shrine or an altar. It's a little square table with a bowl of water and a bowl of clear oil on it. And on the walls on either side of this are two big picture frames with the rules of the dojo in the same kind of writing that's on the sign. One says:

ONE: I will become better, for I am infinitely per-
fectible.
ONE: I will become truthful, for that is strength.
ONE: I will become peaceful, for that is my truest self.

ONE: I will become brave, for fear is almost always un-
          necessary.
ONE: I will become careful with my courage, for it is
          not to be wasted.

The other one says:

The Spirit of the Warrior

To flee rather than fight is honorable.
To fight when flight is impossible is honorable.
To fight in defense of the weak or the truth may be
honorable.
To neither flee nor fight is most honorable.
To fight for its own sake is never honorable.

Victor takes off his shoes. So do Leon and José. So do I. So
does everybody except Blake. He runs out into the middle of
the mats and says, "Hey! Should I take my shoes off?"

Victor walks across the mats to his shrine. He lights the oil
in the bowl and a perfect little flame starts up.

"Come here," he says to Blake.

At first Blake doesn't move. Then he looks into Victor's face,
and he does.

I hear Victor say, almost whispering, "Water is for spirit. Salt
is for the body. Flame is for will. Every day when you come
we will contemplate these things together. Then you will work.
After that, you will join the beginners' class. After that, you will
practice while I teach my other classes. After that, I will take
you home. Every day but Sunday. In the dojo you will call me
sensei. That means teacher. You will bow to me. I will bow to
you. There will be respect between us, always."

"Yeah, right," Blake says. He grins, but he's nervous.

"You think you're bad," Victor goes on. "You think you're
tough. But, *chico,* you don't know what those things are. I do.

I know all about them. The path you are on now is the path I was on. But you do not know the truth of that path. It will destroy you. You are not strong enough for it. It nearly destroyed me, and I am much stronger than you are. But I will show you the path of honor. Honor saved me. It will save you if you follow it. Take off your shoes and join me."

Leon nods his head toward the door. José and I put our shoes back on and we all tiptoe out.

I look back over my shoulder. Blake is taking his time about it, but he's untying his shoes.

23

FACEPLACE

THINGS WERE DIFFERENT at school today. First, two kids I don't
even know came up and said, "You think you're so cool? Well,
you suck. We're gonna get you good." And they walked off.

Which was a surprise. But not as big a surprise as when the
same kind of thing happened three more times before lunch.
What is the universe up to now?

And when José and Laura and I sat together in the cafeteria, nobody sat near us, even though the place was crowded.

Then in gym class I got knocked down from behind when
we were doing jumping jacks.

And in algebra, Tiffany said, "Great Web site, Witch Bitch,"
and then she whispered something that I didn't hear because
if I had heard it I'd have slugged her and that would have got
me into Garbage's office for another Zero Tolerance of Kestrel
session.

Besides, maybe I owed her a pass. Because she gave me a clue
to what was going on. And as soon as I got home I got on the
Web and typed in my name.

You know FacePlace, right? Maybe you don't if you're reading this a hundred years from now. Maybe they have something better. Or worse.

FacePlace is this Internet thing where you post stuff. Make up websites for yourself.

Or for other people. To slam them. Because the beauty part of it is, nobody knows exactly who did it. Except I do know exactly who did it.

Being a witch, I don't have a lot of time for FacePlace. I don't have a site of my own, or anything. I mean, the Craft isn't for every bozo on the bus, as Ariel says.

But today I am there. Big time. At kestrelwitchbitch.com. And the site is a horror.

The homepage says:

Enter and Be Damned.
Join the Spawn of Satan.
Let Kestrel Witchbitch
Take You to Hell!

And there are these flames flickering all around the edges and a picture of me, only it isn't really me because I do not wear red horns on my head, and those are definitely not my breasts bouncing around.

You click on me and you go to this:

Witchbitches Are Cool,
Witchbitches Rule,
Witchbitches Take Over
Your High School

And below that are pictures of the burned part of the school. And I am in every one of them, pointing and grinning. And under the pictures it says things like:

Nobody can make me wear a sucky uniform.
I made them think Blake did it.
Satan rules. Burn the school.
I caste this spell.

And there are other pages. Some of them are old-fashioned woodcuts of witches' sabbaths, or what people in the old days thought witches' sabbaths were like. Some of them are pictures from the school. Some of them are of Laura ("This is my first slave.") Some of them are porn. I am in a lot of them. My face stuck on. Pictures taken of me with cells when I wasn't looking.

The captions say things like:

Hi, I'm Kestrel Murphy. Kestrel the Kool, Witchbitch Number One. Worship me or die. I came to this sucky school (Richard Milhous Nixon Union High) this year. But none of you are cool enough for me. Because I am the Queen of Evil and you don't respect that. So I am going to make you get down on your knees to me with my magic powers. If you don't you will be punished....

There's a slide show, too. When you run it, there's a girl's voice under it that says pretty much the same things.

"You punks are so lame. Everyone who doesn't worship me is lame. I mean, look at this school. So boring. It *needs* to be burned down...."

I look at the whole thing. Then I get to the comments. Which I will not write down. Because they are worse than anything on the site.

And by now I'm crying. I mean, everyone knows this kind of stuff happens. But that doesn't make it okay. Because it's so sneaky. And so unfair. And because I know exactly who did it. Because this is a really good website, and Blake's too dumb to have done the graphics. And because T&A always spelled *wrong* on that note they left on the back of my English book. And because, how do I get them for it? This is not something to say *interesting* about. It's not interesting. It's hell.

The first thing I do is post.

"Hey, this isn't me. This is something a couple of the Queens have done. Got done, because they are too damn stupid to do something complicated like this." And then I go on and say a lot of things about T&A and the Craft and what it really is and by the time I'm done it's about four screens long.

I read it over, because I am not going to have one single spelling mistake or grammar error in this. And then I read it over again. And I do not post it. Because, angry as I am, and right as I am, I can't put in so much about the Craft.

And then Ariel is knocking on the door and telling me it's time for dinner.

"I don't want any!" I holler. And something in my voice, like maybe the fact that I'm crying again, makes her ask,

"May I come in?"

"No," I say, and open the door.

When Ariel knows what's going on, she looks over the site like she's Sherlock Holmes and she's going to catch the Hound of the Baskervilles and neuter him.

When she's done, she says, "It's pretty professional. I wonder if they paid to have it done."

"What difference would that make?" I say.

"It might suggest there's an adult involved," Aunt Ariel says. "Somebody who could afford this kind of work."

"The Queens have money," I say.

"Mmm-hmm. And if they all shared the cost, that could work. But I can't help wondering if someone we both know and love wasn't involved."

"Garbage? You think he'd do something like that?" I say.

"I think he would if he thought he couldn't get caught. Which is probably the case."

Aunt Ariel sits in front of my computer with her hand over

her face. Then she says, "Let's have dinner. Then we'll cast a spell."

And we do. But my stomach isn't in dinner and my heart isn't in the spell. And even though Ariel e-mails FacePlace and tells them the site is about a fourteen-year-old girl and isn't her work and they promise to take it down, I still don't want to go to school tomorrow.

Which is what I have to do.

BLAKE JOINS THE UNIVERSE

THE SITE IS GONE THE NEXT DAY. But the feelings aren't. Not mine. And not anybody else's, either.

Things are okay when I enter the hallowed hells of good ol' Richard Milhous Nixon. For about two seconds. Then somebody slams into me from behind, and says, "Oops," and goes on. It's no one I know, no one I ever saw before.

The same thing happens twice more on my way to first period. If I didn't know better, I would seriously begin to wonder if some people didn't like me.

When second period comes, I only have to go five doors down the hall, so I only get slammed into once.

This time, José sees it.

And José changes into someone else as I watch. I don't know who it is, but it's a little bit Leon and a little bit Victor. And maybe a little bit some Aztec warrior from way back. And it's all in the way he walks over to the guy who slammed into me.

The guy sees it, too.

"Oh. Hey, sorry," he says to me. "I thought you were somebody else."

"Like who?" José says.

"Oh, just some girl I know," the guy says.

I have never realized before how tall José is when he stands up straight.

"Maybe you should stop bumping into girls for fun," he says. "Then you wouldn't make no more stupid mistakes."

The guy stands there. He looks totally geeky and uncool.

"But I'll tell you what you can do, if you like bumping into people," José says. "You can try bumping into guys. You can bump into me if you want to. Want to?"

"I gotta get to class," the guy says.

"That's cool," José says. "Be careful."

And the guy oozes away and down the hall.

"Maybe you'd better wait for me after classes," José says. "I could walk you around, you know?"

"Yeah," I say. "You can do that."

And from then on, I have José and he has my back. And knowing that José has it gives me this warm, glowy feeling that does not go away between classes. In fact, it gets stronger.

But that is by the end of the day, and before that, at lunch, I see that the universe is going crazy trying to figure out how to protect Laura, since even José can't be in two places at once.

Because the universe sends her Blake Cump and Jason Horspool and the rest of Blake's guys.

Blake, who was just un-expelled because Leon and Laura's doctor mom went to Gorringe and told him it was better to have Blake in school than out of it, and made him believe it. So now here he is to protect Laura.

Blake and his guys do not eat lunch with us. They do not even talk to us, except a little to Laura.

But when the three of us sit down together, they sit just down the table from Laura on both sides of her. And José sits beside me, across from Laura. And then one of Blake's guys gets up from where he is and comes over and sits on the other side of me. We have an army.

Well, two armies. That do not like each other. But still, when lunch is over—and it's pretty quiet since we do not want to talk Craft or coven in front of Blake and his guys—Blake gets up from the table and he says, "Hey" to José.

And José says, "Hey."

And it is one of those guy things that is about respect, and they have given it to each other. Like a couple of knights who do not like each other but still bow a little when they pass.

And after that day, the sucky harassment stops. And why it stops just shows you how black and white the universe can get when it wants to. Because even the Queens and their court do not want to mess with Blake.

But if you are reading this a hundred years from now, you are probably asking yourself, "Why did a world-class *pinche* like Blake do something good? Is this not totally out of character for a perverted rat creep from hell without a single good thing about him?"

Yes. Except for one small item. And that is this: Laura's class, one she takes on Thursdays, is at the dojo. And Blake likes Laura.

Blake Cump likes Laura Greenwood. And it's not a new thing. He's liked her since fifth grade. And now he gets to see her at the dojo in her little white beat-you-to-a-bloody-pulp suit. And for the first time in his life, Blake Cump does something good for somebody else.

I know all this because José has a new Blake story for me every day. He tells me them while he's walking me to class, which he keeps doing, and which still gives me the warm glowies.

They are strange stories.

"You know," he says. "I think Victor and Blake are making friends. Victor buys Blake dinner every night before the *coche* takes him home. And he says he wishes he could get Blake out of that family he's in. He says he can't understand how Blake turned out as good as he has, now that he's met the rest of them."

This is disgusting. I never even thought there might be more like Blake.

"Who told his parents they could have more children?" I ask.

"I bet they didn't ask permission," José says.

"Victor and Leon and Mrs. Greenwood are trying to figure something out for him," José says later this week. "Victor says he'd almost be willing to take him. Chris would go along with it, but I don't think it's going to happen. Too many complications."

"Why would somebody want Blake in their house?" I ask.

"Especially when Blake doesn't like Mexicans and Victor doesn't like Anglos," José says. "Weird world."

"They don't?" This surprises me. I always assumed Blake didn't like anybody. And Victor is quiet, but he's always nice.

"Victor likes you and your aunt because she speaks Spanish," José says. "That's about it. And Blake never says anything, but you can just tell. Or maybe you can't, since you're not Mexican. But yeah. They're making friends."

"The universe is getting truly strange."

I hate to admit it, but I am getting curious about Blake. But I will not say this, even to José.

But I can ask Laura, because she's a girl.

"I don't know what I think about him," she says when I call her. "What do you think I should do?"

Nobody ever asked me for boy advice before. I have to think about my answer.

"I mean, I'm grateful to him," Laura says. "But I'm kind of afraid of him, too. I mean, there's a lot of anger in him."

"No kidding," I say, looking at Ratchy, who is running across the floor chasing some invisible mouse thing. "What do your rentz say?"

"Well, that's kind of weird," Laura says. "They sort of like him."

"That goes way past kind of weird and gets into Central

Weirdland," I say. "It is all fifty states of the United States of Weirdland. Don't they know what he's like?"

"Well, you know my mom did all these tests on him and stuff," Laura says. "And it turns out he has a very high IQ, which doesn't impress my mom totally because she thinks IQ scores are mostly bogus—"

"They are?" I interrupt.

"Yes. My mom says there are thirty-two identified categories of human intelligence," Laura says. "IQ scores test for eight. So she says you've got a 75 percent chance of being a genius without it showing up on a standard IQ test."

"There is no way Blake Cump is a genius," I say. "Even the universe isn't that crazy."

"Mom says he's very kinesthetic," Laura goes on. "And our schools aren't set up to teach kinesthetic people. That's part of his problem."

"What's *kinesthetic* mean?" I ask. "Evil?"

"It means he learns through his hands," Laura says. "My mom showed him her woodworking shop last weekend and taught him how to use some of her tools. She said she never saw anybody learn so fast."

"What did he steal?" I want to ask. But I don't. Because there is something in Laura's voice that tells me this would not be a good idea.

"What about your dad?" I say.

"He wrote a poem about him," Laura says. "Dad says it's not very good yet. But he thinks in about five years it might be. Anyway, he says Blake's like a cross between a romantic hero and a puncture weed."

"And that's good?" I say.

"Well, it's not bad," Laura says. "Not all bad, anyway. So, anyway. What do you think I should do?"

We are back to that.

I scrunch my face up, because I do not want to answer this

question. I do not want to answer it because Laura is not going to like my answer. And I do not think I am going to like that.

But just in time, I take a step back. I thinksay, *Interesting.*

"What's the universe telling you?" I ask.

"I don't know. I can't hear it," Laura says. "I was hoping maybe you did."

What do I hear?

I hear the sycamore leaves rustling in the warm breeze in the corner of the yard. I hear Aunt Ariel say some bad words as she hits the wrong key on her computer. I hear Ratchy's feet thumping across the floor. I hear Laura's breathing. I hear mine.

So where's the universe in all this ordinary stuff?

We are all flowing together.

That's what I get.

So what does it mean?

And then I get it. Blake is flowing together now, and what is doing it is not that Victor will kill him if he doesn't or that Leon will make him wish Victor had killed him. No. What is making him flow together is that he has hope for the first time in his creepazoid perverted rat life. And Laura is that hope.

Oh, wow. Sometimes the universe gets too crazy.

But Laura is still waiting for me to tell her what I hear. And she's in my coven. I have to help if I can.

So I say, "Don't take away his hope. But make him work for it."

"Oh," Laura says. "Good. I'm glad the universe thinks so."

And I know that the universe does think so, because it is certainly not what I think.

And I'll bet nobody ever paid so much attention to Blake Cump in his life. Which would probably make him very happy if he knew about it, which he never will.

25

BROWNIES

SATURDAY COMES. It is the second one in October, and although it is still hot in Jurupa, there is a feeling of fall in the breeze, and the shadows under the sycamore are a little darker.

José and I decide to celebrate by making brownies. I do not even like brownies. But they are easy, and they are José's favorite. And I am so happy to feel a change in the weather that we end up making about six pans full of them.

That is way too many even for José. So I say, "Man, this is a mess of brownies. Why don't we take them down to the dojo? Do you think Victor would like that?'

"Maybe," José says. "If we don't interrupt anything."

"I would never interrupt," I say. Which is true. The last thing I want is to stop Victor from demonstrating the Aztec death grip or something. Especially if he's using Blake for a model. So we get on our bikes, and I have the brownies in my backpack.

"There's no place to chain up our bikes," José says when we get there. "I'll wait out here."

I walk into the dojo just as there's this huge shout.

"Kiai!"

And a bunch of little kids are in lines, making like Ratchy, fighting the invisible bad guys. They flash like stars in their white uniforms on the blue mat.

Blake is sweeping around the edges of the room. I see he's really careful with that broom. He's getting into corners, reaching up to the ceiling to get cobwebs. There's something serious about him.

Then he sees me and grins like a perverted rat.

He comes over. I stiffen.

"I get to do the bathrooms next," he whispers. "Want to watch me clean a toilet?"

"Thanks, some other time," I say. "Like never." But then I say, "That was cool what you did about Laura. Thanks."

"I was really bummed when the Queens said you set the fire," he answers. "That was one of my best freakouts ever. And they gave you the credit." Then he says, "Well, better get back to work. Otherwise *el jefe* will use me to demonstrate the Aztec death grip again."

I grin, but not at Blake. At the universe. Because how many times do you think or say or hear the words *Aztec death grip* in an average day? Or life? So I know that it's a signal from the universe that it is flowing in a good way now.

The spell Ariel and I cast worked. The universe made Blake Laura's protector. Heck, the universe was already setting this up back when they were in fifth grade.

Way to go, universe, I thinksay.

I take a step back. *Interesting.*

And I understand why I have made the brownies.

I take a piece of paper out of my backpack and write FOR THE DOJO on it, and I put it on the brownies. Then I take another, write FOR VICTOR on it, and wrap up one of the two biggest brownies. Then I take a third, write FOR BLAKE on it, and wrap up another humungous one. And I say, "Blessèd be," and I leave.

STICKS

This has been Stick Week.

Tuesday, I get called into Garbage's office. His head looks bigger and more like a basketball than usual. I wonder if his collar is too tight.

But he has not brought me down there to see his latest fashion statement. T&A are there. They look scared. Garbage looks mad.

"Ms. Murphy," Garbage says. "You are here to explain these."

He holds out some little figures made of sticks. They look like the kind of people first-graders draw, except they have no heads. They are held together with really complicated knots.

"Nice knots," I say.

"And are you the one who tied them?" Garbage asks me.

T&A inhale like they're afraid. *Bogus,* I think. But their eyes really do look scared.

"Nope."

"Then who did?" Garbage leans forward. He makes his little

temple with his hands and looks at me over it. *The Temple of Garbage,* I think, and try not to laugh.

"Somebody else," I say. "Just my guess."

"These were in our lockers," Tiffany shouts. "Hanging up by their necks."

"Oh, poor little sticks," I say. "What a tragic way to die."

"Was this an attempt to put a curse on these girls?" Garbage asks.

"Don't ask me," I say. "That isn't my thing."

"Then whose 'thing' is it?" Garbage practically shouts.

"I don't know," I say. "But I do have a theory. Look for somebody who knows how to break into lockers and get away with it." And I jerk my head toward T&A.

They let out a couple of yelps like I just stepped on their toes.

"You did this to us," Amber insists. "Everybody else likes us."

Now I do laugh. "Practically any kid in this school would have done this if they could have," I say.

"That's not true! We're popular," says Tiffany.

And Garbage says, "I tell you frankly, Ms. Murphy, that if you did not do this, I think you know exactly who did."

"Then ask me and I'll tell you," I say. "A witch never lies."

"Who did it?" Garbage says.

"I don't know," I say. "But I have an idea. If you two are really so scared of a couple of sticks, let me do a protection spell for you. Like the one my aunt and I did to keep you off of Laura Greenwood."

"No," Tiffany says.

"You keep your spells and things off us," Amber says.

"Just trying to help."

"Return to your classroom, Ms. Murphy. You have been warned," Garbage says.

Yeah, I have. But about what? For the rest of the day I am wondering about those stick thingies.

Wednesday comes and I am back in Garbage's office again. This time T&A have found the little stick guys in their gym bags.

There's more hollering from them and from Garbage. But what can they do? Especially after I offer to cast a protection spell for them again. Back to class for me.

But the same thing happens Thursday. Stick girls in their backpacks. Then in their lockers again.

By now I am almost as anxious as they are to know who is doing this.

Friday comes. Spirit Assembly. And Garbage gives the fantastic plastic to the latest suck-up. Then he says, "And now I have to discuss a very serious situation. I am sure many of you already know what I am about to refer to. I refer to this." And he holds up one of the little danglies.

"Someone has been using these objects to terrorize certain students in this school," Garbage goes on. "It will not be tolerated. It is a form of violence. And this school stands by its zero-tolerance policy. If anyone has information on who is committing these acts, come to my office with it. Your confidentiality will be assured."

There's a buzz in the cafetorium. Whispers asking "What is it…? Terrorism…? What's terroristic about that thing?"

And some kid in the back calls, "Can't see it. Hold it up."

Garbage does. He stretches his arm up as high as it will reach, but it doesn't make the little stick thingy any bigger.

"Still can't see it," says another voice.

Then, "Higher!"

And then somebody wails, "Oh, my God, it's a stick! Help! Save me!"

And a long slow wave of laughter starts at the back of the cafetorium and wanders up to the front.

"This is a serious matter," Garbage says.

"It's a serious stick!" someone shouts, and runs out of the cafetorium screaming and waving his arms over his head.

It's Jason Horspool.

And then the big laugh comes.

"Be quiet, be quiet," Garbage is shouting.

Teachers are holding up their hands and one of the coaches is blowing his whistle.

By now the place is starting to come apart.

And that's when Laura gets up and walks onto the stage and says into the microphone, "Excuse me, Mr. Gorringe. I know who's been making those figures."

That gets people interested. Slowly, they quiet down. The coach stops blowing his whistle.

Garbage says, "Please come to my office with this information."

But Laura says, "I'm afraid not, sir. It's very important."

She's pretty far away from me, but I think she's trembling. I can hear her voice shaking. But she's like that little dancer statue she brings to coven. She's not moving.

She says, "I did it."

Now it gets a lot quieter. Everyone sits down. Even the teachers.

"A while ago, the Queens did something very mean to someone they didn't like," she goes on. "I told on the ones who'd done it. You can guess what happened next. They started to leave me notes. Everywhere. Every day. Threats. You know the kind of things they do. Then they put up that Web site."

"That's enough," says Garbage. "I'll see you in my office."

But just as he takes the microphone away, Laura grabs it and says, "So I was worrying about what they were going to do next. And I told a friend, and he said I should try this. And he helped me do it. And these sticks aren't spells or anything. They're just sticks. The Queens are apparently afraid of sticks."

Some people laugh. Some clap. Most just sit there.

Laura hands the microphone back to Garbage and leaves the stage.

"Way to go, Laura," someone calls out, and there is more clapping.

"This assembly is dismissed," Garbage shouts.

So I'm pushing along through the hall and hearing giggles about sticks and wondering why Laura didn't say anything about this to me, when José comes up beside me.

"Want one?" he says.

It's a little stick guy on a loop. José already has one around his neck.

"You knew about this, too," I say.

"Yeah," he says. "Me, Laura, Blake, and Blake's guys."

"Well, why didn't you tell me?" I ask.

"So you wouldn't get in trouble," José says. "Duh."

"Oh. Yeah. That works. Thanks," I say.

"It didn't work out how we planned it," he says. "It was supposed to go on longer. Laura getting up there was her own idea. But I think it worked out better."

I take the little guy and hang him from my neck.

"Whose idea was it first?" I say.

"Well, yours, kind of," José says. "Laura starts telling Blake how scared she is of the Queens, and he gets all mad. But he knows Laura won't like him if he does anything really mean. Plus, they're at the dojo. So he tries to think 'What's honorable?'"

"No way!" I say.

"Way," José tells me. "So he comes to me and we talk. And then Blake gets the idea, and I think, 'This is what Kestrel meant. Using our majix to help each other.' So Blake teaches me how to tie the knots and we start making them. And Laura helps, and pretty soon we have almost a hundred. And maybe Jason breaks into the Queens' lockers and leaves them there. Anyway, now we're going to pass them out to every kid that wants one."

That afternoon, we spend our time in the coven making them. When I tell Ariel what's going on, she laughs and gets some of her coven in on it. All weekend long, a bunch of us make little stick dollies guaranteed to frighten the Queens.

By the end of Monday, half the kids in school are wearing them.

Tuesday there's a message from Garbage. "Stick figures are not authorized to be worn with the school uniform."

Wednesday, which is today, practically every kid in school is wearing a stick around his neck. That's it. Just a stick.

And when the teachers say to take them off, the kids say, "Why can't I wear a stick? This school has zero tolerance for sticks?"

And one of the girls has a father who works for the newspaper. And he does an article about it. And then one of the TV stations picks it up.

HERE'S WHAT WAS ON

TV WOMAN: This is Richard Milhous Nixon Union High School where the administration is being plagued by an onset of sticks. That's right—sticks. Students are taking to wearing sticks around their necks as a symbol of—well, let's ask one of the students just what it is a symbol of. This is Coventry Squires, a fifteen-year-old sophomore. Coventry, why are you wearing a stick around your neck?

COVENTRY: 'Cause wearing a steering wheel around my neck would look stupid.

TV WOMAN: But why a stick?

COVENTRY: It's cooler than a whole tree.

TV WOMAN: This is Luís Sandoval, who also wears a stick around his neck. Luís, what does the stick mean to you?

LUÍS: It doesn't mean anything, man. That's the point. Get it?

TV WOMAN: Your principal, Mr. Gorringe, says that the sticks are an occult satanic symbol. What do you say?

LUÍS: I say what's an occulp—what you said?

GIRL: Hi, I'm Monica Whitman, and I have a stick, too!

TV WOMAN: How about you, young lady? Does your stick have any special meaning?

GIRL: Of course. Every stick is special. I mean, there's no two alike, you know?

TV WOMAN: And now for the administration's point of view. We spoke to Principal Dewayne Gorringe. Principal Gorringe, why are you so concerned about the presence of sticks around your students' necks?

GARBAGE: The wearing of sticks began very recently and is the outgrowth of an attempt by a small group of students to terrorize another group by the use of witchcraft. This school has a zero-tolerance policy and sticks will not be tolerated.

TV WOMAN: Sticks are a kind of witchcraft?

GARBAGE: At this school, they are.

TV WOMAN: Can you explain how that works?

GARBAGE: Some people feel that the sticks have an occult power to harm other students.

TV WOMAN: The students we talked to said they were just sticks.

GARBAGE: The sticks were originally much more elaborate figures. I have an example here.

And Garbage reaches into his desk and pulls out one of Blake's little guys. But an arm has come off and so has a little stick that was supposed to be a head. It doesn't look like much.

TV WOMAN: This is supposed to be satanic?

GARBAGE: It may not look like it, now, but when I first saw it, believe me, it did.

TV WOMAN: Some students are saying that the sticks are actually a protest against the behavior of a particular group of socially prominent students and don't have anything to do with witchcraft or satanism. What do you say to that?

GARBAGE: They may be honestly mistaken. In some cases. But I know witchcraft when I see it.

TV WOMAN: How?

GARBAGE: I'm a trained professional.

TV WOMAN: Not a professional witch, presumably.

GARBAGE: No, I am the principal of this high school.

TV WOMAN: And there you have it. Are the sticks a protest, a joke, or the emblem of a satanic cult? What do the kids at Nixon High say?

A HUGE BUNCH OF KIDS IN FRONT OF THE SCHOOL: We want our sticks!

Which just goes to show me how twisted the universe can get. I mean, when Ariel and I cast Laura's protection spell, I sure didn't mean that the universe should use Blake to carry it out. But that's what's happened.

   Interesting.

SAMHAIN

GORRINGE STILL MAKES US take off our sticks. The board of education backs him up.

Laura gets a week of detention.

Her first day, I make more brownies and take her one.

"Thanks." She smiles. "I feel so proud of myself. And my father is bragging about me to his classes."

Then I go down to the dojo and take one to Blake.

"Brownies again?" he says when I give it to him. "The last one you left me practically killed me."

I smile. "Just for that, I'm going to bring you one every day this week, *pinche*. 'Til you die."

The stick story gets on national TV. It gets on the Web. It gets in more newspapers. And pretty soon, everybody in America knows that Garbage Gorringe is an idiot. Then some late-night comic makes a dumb mistake, looks into the camera, and says in a Garbagey voice, "Don't worry, folks. I'm a trained professional."

And after that, everybody is saying it whenever they screw up.

"I am a trained professional."

And out of nowhere come bumper stickers:

I AM A TRAINED PROFESSIONAL
DON'T STICK IT TO THE KIDS
I AM A STICK OWNER—AND I VOTE

By Samhain, Garbage is famous. But he does not like it.

Samhain is what witches call Halloween. (It is pronounced SOW-en if you ever want to pronounce it.) For us it is a very big deal. Christmas, Halloween, and New Year's Eve all wrapped up in one night. Plus, this year the moon is going to be full right on the Night. A true harvest moon. Very big deal.

Now I was going to have a ceremony with my coven. Only it turns out that Laura promised six months ago to help out with a little kids' party on Halloween. Which means me and José. Except he's got some family thing to go to that he can't get out of. So I figure Aunt Ariel will cut some slack for her favorite niece and let me join her ceremony.

So I say, "You know, Aunt Ariel, best of witches, it's almost Samhain."

"Tomorrow night," she says.

"Well, it turns out I'm not busy," I say.

And Aunt Ariel looks a little weird, like she's about to say something she can't believe she's going to say, and says it anyway. "Well. You know the Rule of Thirteen."

"Oh," I say, like I'd forgotten it. "Yeah."

And I'm quiet because I know that she means that since her coven has exactly thirteen witches, WE aren't doing anything tomorrow night.

"I'm very sorry, Kestrel," Aunt Ariel says. "Perhaps I could ask one of the others not to come."

"No," I say. "That would be way unfair."

Ariel nods. "You're right. It would."

"It's cool," I tell her, and I get up from the table to do the dishes.

Then I do my homework. This is supposed to help me not to think about Samhain, but it doesn't. I think about TV, but who needs that? It's all about people sitting around in their living rooms with their friends.

Then I think, *majix this. Duh.*

I go into my room, get out this book and doodle around for a while, waiting for a spell to come. It doesn't take long until one does:

> *Samhain, I am all alone,*
> *Bring me help by telephone.*

Then I get out my pentagram and say the chant at all five points. I burn some incense, too. Now it's just a matter of waiting to see how the universe flows.

I'm waiting for the universe in the kitchen with a couple of cookies when my cell rings. I check who's calling. José.

Ah, yes, I was expecting him, I thinksay.

HERE'S HOW JOSÉ HELPED THE UNIVERSE

José: Hey, Kestrel, I heard Laura can't come to your thing, either. Want to come to my thing?

ME: What is it?

José: The little kids go trick-or-treating and the adults have an *ofrenda*. Afterwards there's a party.

ME: I'm there. What time?

I don't even ask what an *ofrenda* is. Who cares? I'm invited to it.

José: Oh, yeah. Ariel can come, too.

ME: She's busy. But I'll be there.

José: Okay if we pick you up about six?

ME: Sure.

We hang up and I tell Aunt Ariel, "It's cool. The universe is sending me to José's for Samhain. What's an *ofrenda?*"

"Did you ever hear of the Day of the Dead?" Ariel asks.

"It's like Mexican Halloween," I say.

"You could say that," Ariel says. "Anyway, an *ofrenda* is a memorial altar. But are they doing one at Halloween?"

"Yeah," I say.

"Hmm," says Aunt Ariel. "It's usually one day later, on All Souls' Day."

"Too bad," I say. "If it was, you could go."

"Yeah," she says. "And I'm really sorry I can't."

But I am totally happy. My Samhain is taken care of, and my spell has worked. I write it down here in my book of majix.

28

MY OWN PERSONAL SKULL

I AM ALL READY WHEN JOSÉ comes to get me. I stand on the front lawn and watch the first little kids going up and down the street in their costumes. Their rentz are walking with them. It makes me miss mine, a little. Mommy Angel used to take me around when I was little, and BD would always bring home some candy just for me. Don't ask me how he could always remember Halloween. He just did. It was a universe thing, I guess.

But now there is no more time for sad because the *coche* pulls up and away we go.

When we get to José's street it's full of trick-or-treaters. I see Chris with a bunch of kids around him going door-to-door and women passing out candy.

We go along with Chris's bunch hanging back and being cool, and it is way cool to be one of the big ones looking out for the little ones.

The moon is huge, like it's never been this big before. It is also orange. The smog colors it that. It looks like this big, squashed jack-o'-lantern. What could be better for Samhain?

"Too bad your aunt couldn't come," Chris says.

"That's what she thinks," I say.

Up and down the street we go, to all seven houses. Then we go a few streets over, and then it is time to start herding the little ones back home.

When we get back to the Iturrigarays' street, the garage door to Leon's house is open, and what I see there I have never seen before. The whole thing is full of flowers from the gardens around the houses on this street. At the back, they reach almost to the ceiling. Others are hanging down from the rafters to meet them. A carpet is spread on the floor. It is old, but pretty. And standing on the carpet is a big table, covered with stuff. There are pictures of people, and bunches of marigolds, and little piles of things, like old tobacco tins and rosary beads. There are skulls made of sugar with names spelled on their foreheads. I see LEON, CHRIS, VICTOR, JOSÉ, and a lot of others. I guess there's one for everybody in the family.

"This is the *ofrenda,*" José says. He sort of points with his chin. "That's my father."

I see an old colored photograph in a big leather frame. There's a guy in a uniform with a flag behind him. He's got a helmet on his head.

"He was airborne," José says. "In Vietnam."

"What was his name?" I ask.

"Armando. Like on the *coche,*" José says.

People come up and talk to the pictures and leave flowers and candles in front of them. The older people are explaining to the little ones who the people in the pictures are. When the little ones have said hello to everybody on the altar, they take the candy skulls with their names on them, but they don't eat them. Not yet. They are still in their costumes, all the little ghosts and princesses and aliens, running around about waist-high to the rest of us, and they are laughing and full of candy, and us old ones are more serious and some of us are crying.

I just look at this wonderful thing the Iturrigarays have made to remember José's father and all these other people who were part of their lives.

"I got to go say hello," José says when the crowd has thinned out.

"You want to introduce me?" I say.

"Come on," he says. And takes my hand real lightly.

"Papi, this is Kestrel Murphy," he says to the picture.

"Blesséd be, Mr. Iturrigaray," I say.

José takes this big breath and says, "I'm doing okay in school, Papi. Kestrel's helping me with English, and my drawing is good."

"His drawing is way better than good," I put in.

Doña Imelda is sitting beside the *ofrenda,* and her eyes are shining and dark. She leans over and says something in Spanish.

"She says, 'The wall between the worlds is very thin to-night,'" José tells me.

And then this totally great weird feeling happens and it's like all the time there ever was is happening right now. And all the people there ever were are right around me, and it's scary but not, all at the same time.

"Yeah," I say. "You're right, señora."

José picks up his skull. It is pink, with his name in red. Then he hands me one that was at the back. White with blue letters. KESTREL.

He leads me back, and Chris goes up.

"José, there's one thing I have to know," I say. "How come you put live people's names on these skulls?"

"'Cause someday we're going to be in one of those pictures," he says.

I go outside onto the driveway and stand in the shadows of the front yard. The moon has climbed above the smog now and is as white and blue as the skull in my hands. And it is like it knows I'm here, and it is blessing me, wanting me to be happy.

José comes up beside me. I feel the warm glowies come back, bright and warm as the *ofrenda* candles.

And I put my hand out, and my hand is attached to my arm, and my arm is attached to the rest of me, and he takes it and I take his and we wrap them around each other and we kiss.

And I am happy. So happy that it's like it's not really just my happiness. It belongs to the whole universe.

THE WALL BETWEEN THE WORLDS

W<small>HICH LASTS UNTIL</small> I <small>GET HOME.</small>

The *coche* purrs away from the curb and I wave until the night takes it in.

When I come into the house, Ratchy runs out and pounces on me. I pick him up, but he wants to fight, so I play with him to wear him out. Then he hops up on a chair and goes to sleep.

Aunt Ariel isn't home yet, but it is way short of midnight, so I don't expect her. Anyway, it is nice to have the house all to myself. I can't believe how grown-up I feel, wandering all over the house in the dark, feeling it is mine, feeling that I really belong here.

Then Ariel's phone rings.

I don't pick it up the first time. I figure at this time of night it has to be for her. But then it rings again about ten minutes later, and again a little after that. Whoever it is is leaving messages. I decide I'd better listen.

There is a whole stream of them, starting about eight o'clock. All from Mommy Angel. Here is the first one: "Susan, dear. This is your mother. You'd better come home at once. It's your father—he's had another attack. He's back in the hospital. I'm—afraid it's pretty bad—" and she starts to sob.

I listen to all the other messages, but they don't say anything but, "Please pick up the phone," and "Please call as soon as you get home," and stuff like that. There's no more news.

So I call.

But there's no answer. Not at home. Not on Mommy Angel's cell phone.

I get scared. It's like I hear Doña Imelda saying, "The wall between the worlds is very thin tonight." I sit down on the floor and start to cry. I am still crying when Ariel gets home.

She's all happy and smells like cinnamon and incense, but as soon as she sees me she gets a totally scared look. She sits down on the floor and holds me.

"My daddy's sick" is all I can get out.

We try for another hour to get Mommy Angel on the phone before she finally calls us. When she does, it turns out that she accidentally turned her cell phone off, and she was too busy to call back anyway.

"They're operating right now," she says. "It's a blood clot in his heart. Susan, you'd better come home."

"Okay," I say. This is no time to remind her that my name is Kestrel.

"She'll be on the first plane out," Ariel says, and I am.

WHEN MOMMY ANGEL MEETS ME at the airport, she looks gray and her eyes are tired and scared.

"Do I look as bad as you do?" I say.

"I've been up all night," she says.

"Me, too," I say.

We hug like we never hugged before and like we think we never will again. It feels so good.

"When can I see Daddy?" I ask.

"He's still in intensive care. No visitors," she says. "Do you want breakfast?"

"Ariel made me eat before I left," I say. "I wasn't hungry. I don't feel like I'll ever be hungry again."

"I know," Mommy Angel says. "I feel the same way."

We go home. On the way, Mommy Angel tells me what happened.

Daddy just fell over when he was walking on his new treadmill. If Mommy Angel hadn't been home, he would have died right then. But the paramedics came in time and got his heart going again. They found the blood clot at the hospital. It is so big they're surprised he's still alive.

"But he's all right now," I say. "He's going to be all right, right?"

Mommy Angel doesn't answer right away. "He's over this one," she says. "There may be other blood clots. Any one of them is very serious."

"Like it could kill him serious?" I ask, even though I know the answer.

"Yes," she says after a minute.

I start crying again and I don't stop until we get home.

It is totally weird to be back. Everything looks smaller, even our house, which is huge. Especially the house. What's weirder is that everything feels familiar and strange at the same time. A couple of times I turn around and am surprised that Ariel's not there. Once I think I feel Ratchy pulling at my shoelace, but it's only me stepping on it. I am like in two places at once. Or maybe nowhere.

Finally, I sit down in a chair to rest for a few minutes. The next thing I know, it's two hours later and the phone is ringing.

It's the hospital. Daddy is doing okay. If he is still doing okay tomorrow, they'll move him out of intensive care and we can visit him.

I call Ariel and tell her. When I hear her voice, it's like it's more real than Mommy Angel's voice, even though she's in the room with me. I miss that voice. I need it.

"The coven is meeting tonight," she says. "We're going to do a healing for him. Is there anything I can do for you, darling?"

"Have you got a picture of Daddy?" I ask.

"Yes," Ariel says.

"Then give it to José and tell him I need him to draw Daddy being healthy," I say. "He'll know what to do."

"Good idea," Ariel says.

"And ask him to ask Doña Imelda about the wall between the worlds. I need to know if it's getting thicker.... And tell Ratchy—"

I stop. What am I supposed to tell Ratchy? Am I going back to Ariel when this is over? Am I ever going to see José again? I just stay on the phone not wanting to hang up and break the connection to everything down in ugly old Jurupa.

Finally, Ariel says, "I'll tell Ratchy not to worry."

"Okay," I say.

"Now call me any time you need me, Kestrel. Understand?" Ariel says.

"Yeah."

But I still don't hang up.

Ariel waits for me and finally she says, "Bléssed be."

"Bléssed be," I say, and I do hang up.

But nothing feels bléssed.

SALUD, PESETAS, Y AMOR

HERE IS WHAT THERE IS ABOUT HOSPITALS THAT MAKES THEM HOSPITALS

1. The smell. No place else smells like a hospital. They smell like something terrible is happening and they are trying to cover it up.
2. Something terrible is happening and they are trying to cover it up.
3. The light at night looks like you are inside a bad spaceship.
4. Half the stuff looks like it is warm and soft, or is supposed to be warm and soft. The rest of it looks like equipment on a *really* bad spaceship.
5. When a fire starts in one of the rooms, they say, "Dr. Red: Room Whatever It Is" so you won't know the hospital's about to burn down with you in it.

HERE IS HOW I KNOW THAT

It is three days before they finally let us see him. When they do, Mommy Angel and I are walking down the hall to his room when we hear "Dr. Red" come over the intercom and everybody starts running to room 331. Which is Daddy's.

This guy who is pushing a wheelchair leaves the chair, grabs a fire extinguisher off the wall, runs into Daddy's room, and sprays his wastebasket, which is burning like a torch. Everybody is really scared because there is oxygen in that room, and it could have exploded!

It was the guy next to my daddy who'd started the fire. He'd tried to light a cigarette and dropped the match. Clever.

Mommy Angel is furious. The look in her eyes could peel paint off walls. She rips those hospital guys up one side and down the other for letting that guy sneak cigarettes. I didn't know she could talk like that. If words could start fires by themselves, those hospital guys would be torched. And they don't even try to answer her back. Because she is right.

And I am very proud of her.

"Mom, I didn't know you could do that," I say when she is done and it is just the three of us in the room because El Cigaretto is Out of There. Because Mommy Angel tells them to get his ass out NOW and that is what they do with it.

"Honey, I worked in nightclubs from the time I was seventeen. What you just heard was nothin'," she says in her best Virginia Lady accent.

"Oh, yes it was."

But Daddy just says, "Looks like those damn things are going to get me one way or another."

"The hell they are," my mother says, and I know she is casting a spell on him.

And BD laughs a little.

Big Daddy laughing? He doesn't. Ever.

Then he holds out a hand to me and says, "Hello, baby. Hello, Kestrel."

So I take his hand. It is clammy and soft and weak, but it is his. And he is still here to hold it out to me. For a minute, I am Daddy's little girl again.

They put him into a wheelchair—and whoever came up with those hospital nightgowns should be made to wear one for the rest of his life and see how he likes it—and we went down to the cafeteria while they cleaned up the room.

"How are you feeling?" I say.

"Pretty good for a guy with phlebitis and two heart attacks, who's just been nearly burned to death or blown up," Daddy says slowly. "I'm looking forward to going home."

"What's the first thing you want to do?" I say.

"Sit under the trees," Daddy says.

This does not sound like BD. I was pretty sure he didn't know we had trees. I am a little surprised that he knows what trees are. But he goes on.

"We get a lot of birds, don't we?" he says. "I want to look at them. You know I don't know the name of a single bird? I mean, to look at. I know words, like *robin* and *blue jay*. But I have no idea what they actually look like. Do we have robins or blue jays?"

"Robins *and* blue jays," I say.

"Good," he says. "How about hawks and eagles and sea-gulls?"

"Not in the yard," I say, before I see he is yanking my chain. "But we do get ostriches."

"Good," he says. "I really want to see some ostriches."

Up to now, Mommy Angel hasn't said anything but the usual things, which is why I haven't put any of them down. But now she says something worth writing. She says, "Ted, I really, really love you," and her eyes are shiny and her hands are tight on his.

"I don't see how you can," he says after a minute. "But I'm glad you still do. I'll make it worth your time from now on."

"It was always worth my time," she says. But he interrupts.

"This is the best thing that's ever happened to us," he says. "The best thing that's ever happened to *us*. It's going to change our lives. I'm going to learn how to enjoy things. All kinds of things. There's an old Spanish saying I heard somewhere— *salud, pesetas, y amor, y tiempo para gozarlos.* It means 'health, money, love, and time to enjoy them.' And that's exactly what we've got, except for my health, and I can work on that."

"I didn't know your knew any Spanish," says Mommy Angel.

BD shrugs. The way I do.

"But Mommy Angel is right," I say. "It is truly weird for you to talk like that. In any language."

"Push me up the hall, Kestrel," Daddy says. "I want to talk to you."

Uh-oh. A lecture about calling Mommy Angel Mommy Angel.

But then he says, "I want to ask you something."

So I push him out into the hall.

It is hard to push a wheelchair. It steers a little better than a shopping cart, but not much. And Daddy is heavy for me.

On the ground floor, where the cafeteria is, there is a door that leads to a little park surrounded by the hospital. Daddy asks me to take him out there. I park him beside a concrete bench that says In Memory of Wilhelmina Everson, and sit on Wilhelmina's name.

Remind me never to buy a memorial bench at a hospital.

"How are you and Ariel getting along?" he says. "Really?"

"Great," I say. "She is way cool. I miss her."

Daddy says, "I never really understood what she was all about. Maybe I can get to know her better now. And maybe she can help me understand a few things."

"Like what?" I say, all surprised.

For a long time Daddy doesn't answer. Then he says, "That night the blood clot lodged in my heart I nearly died. You know that. What I haven't told anybody yet is what happened to me when they were working on me."

He doesn't look at me. He wants to talk, but he's embarrassed.

"I was somewhere, but I didn't know where. It was dark and all I knew was I didn't want to be there, but I couldn't leave. I didn't know the way out. And if I took one wrong step, I could never get out. Never come back. I don't know how long I was there. Time didn't have any meaning. But then someone was with me. I know I had never seen this guy before. He smiled at me, and put his hands on my shoulders and spun me around and said, 'That way, *ese*. And keep going.' And then he said, '*salud, pesetas, y amor, y tiempo para gozarlos*—health, money, love, and time to enjoy them.' And I knew he was sending me back to you."

I just sit there all tingly and dizzy. Then Daddy says, "There's one more thing. Really strange. He was wearing some kind of uniform. Helmet, boots, patches all over his jacket. Kind of old-fashioned. Like World War II."

"Not World War II," I say. "Vietnam."

SO I TELL DADDY ABOUT SAMHAIN and the *ofrenda* and the wall between the worlds.

He shakes his head. "I can't believe it," he says. "But what else can I believe?" Then he says, "What do you think Alice would say about this?"

"I think she might say something like, 'Probably the best thing to do about the universe is to be grateful for it,'" I say.

"And what would you say?" Daddy asked me.

"The same," I say.

"That sounds good," Daddy says. "Feels right. I think I can do it. Wheel me back in to my beautiful wife."

And we leave Wilhelmina the Concrete Bench where she is. And my heart is glowing because I know my Daddy is going to live.

Three days later they let Daddy come home.

HERE'S WHAT WAS DIFFERENT

1. Just about everything.
2. Daddy sat in the backyard and watched the sun set.

3. He had me and Mommy Angel go to the store and buy a feeder and a bath for the birds.
4. He started reading a book that was not about computers or money. Something Aunt Ariel sent him.
5. After they talked on the phone.
6. He was always looking at Mommy Angel and she was always looking at him.
7. And she started wearing soft-looking things and moving slower.
8. And here's the big one. Mommy Angel turned out to be totally not interested in catalogs or shopping or anything but what was going on with BD and me. And that was good because BD needed all of it, and I liked it, too.

And here's what the universe gave me: sometimes a person needs another person to be all dependent on them and they are. And then things change and the first person is the one who needs to be all dependent and the second person takes over the take-care stuff. And you find out that the second person was always really like this underneath, they just didn't do it because the first person was so important to them. And that's my Rentz.

HERE'S WHAT WAS NOT DIFFERENT

Mommy Angel was still singing her old songs. Especially,

When love flies out the window
The best thing you can do
Is keep the window open
'Til it flies back to you.

And I get for the first time (D'OH) that what she's singing about is what she's thinking about, really feeling. Which I should have figured out years ago.

And Daddy figures it out, too.

Then I get this envelope from José. It is a picture of my father laughing, smiling, throwing out his arms like he feels great. And he's so real it's like he's ready to get off the page and run around the room. With it is a letter:

Dear Kestrel,
I hope this helps your dad feel better. I did the best I could on it. In fact, this was my third try. Hope you're back soon.
   Anyway, when you do get back, Garbage will be gone. It turned out his big doctor's degree was a fake. The school board made him resign.

[Way to go, universe.]

I've been over to see Ratchy a few times. He's getting big fast. When he sees me he makes this noise that is maybe "Hi" and maybe means "Where is she, you estúpido? Go and get her."
English is okay, but no fun anymore.
Blake gave me this to give to you.
I hope everything comes out okay and you come back soon.
Regards,
José

Something from Blake? Too weird. It's a piece of notebook paper. On the inside is some really big printing in red, black, and orange.

Hey, Kestrel,
Sensei told me about your old man. Just want to say I'm sorry. Hope he doesn't die or anything. Your aunt found out Garbage's big degree was fake and told the school board. RIGHTUOUS. I didn't know she was soo kewl.
Blake Cump

*Oh, yeah. Karate is weird. A lot of it is just sitting. But the dojo's
a good place. I like it better than anywhere else. Someday when
you come back I will brake a brick on my head for you. Or maybe
one of your brownies. HAHA.*
Blake Cump

And with Blake's letter was a little pale pink piece of paper
folded over. It was from Laura.

Dear Kestrel,
*I miss you. So do my rentz, José and his mom, Blake, Ratchy,
and Ariel. And a lot of people at school have asked me about you
and when you are coming back. So when are you coming? José
and I met for coven, but it wasn't the same without you. Blake
asked me if he could come, but I told him it was up to you because you're our head witch. (Is that the right term?) I don't know
how majix he is. But he helps me with mine.*
Please come back soon.
Love,
Laura

TIME WAS PASSING. It had been about two weeks already. The
days were still warm, but the nights were getting cold. And I
wasn't in school or anything. So I thought maybe I had better
mention that. And that night, I did.

"You know," I say, "if I'm going to stay up here, maybe we
should think about sending me to school someplace."

"Aren't you enjoying your time with us?" Mommy Dearest
says. "I'm certainly enjoying having you home."

"Sure," I say. "I just thought you might want me to graduate
someday."

"I suppose you're right," Daddy says. "It's just so great having
you around all the time. Trying to figure out who you are and
who you're turning in to. And what you'll get up to next."

"Who, me?" I say. Then I blush like some kind of dweeb.

"Where would you like to be?" Mommy Angel says. "Up here or down there?"

"I want her up here," Daddy says.

"I think we can let Kestrel decide," Mommy Angel says. "We've been treating her as a problem and not as a person for a long time. Let's let her choose what to do next."

Wow. I'm going to have to stop calling Mom Mommy Angel.

And Daddy says, "Yeah. I guess so."

So I think very, very hard. I think about Ratchy and José and Ariel. I think about the smog and the heat down in Jurupa. I think about Blake and Laura and all the Iturrigarays. I think about my Rentz, and how much I want to be near them. Either way, I am going to end up missing somebody a lot.

I can feel the universe slowing, getting deeper, building up some energy, waiting for the flow to go on.

Finally, I feel it move.

"I'm staying," I say. "But I want to go down and visit a lot. I've got things to do down there."

Daddy hugs me and says, "Thank you, baby. Thank you, Kestrel."

And Mom smiles and hugs us both.

So I call Ariel and tell her. And I call José and Laura and tell them. And we are all kind of sad about it. As in, Ariel cries and so do I. But it feels like what the universe needs.

Ariel sends Ratchy. He is already more than twice as big as when I got him. When he moves in, he starts out sleeping on my bed. He is a good familiar and knows what I need from him. In less than a week, he is sleeping on Daddy for his afternoon naps.

"I have decided that you are never fully dressed without cat hair," Daddy says.

He makes Daddy laugh, too. Once, when we are all gone for a day, Ratchy goes into the kitchen as soon as we come back, and starts whapping on things. Finally, he knocks a cup onto the floor and smashes it.

"There," he looks at us. "That's what I was trying to say."

And Daddy laughs, even though it is his own personal coffee cup.

And I go back to school and it's not bad. It's not anything, really. It's just school. I think about starting a new coven, but I don't really want to. I want my old one back. I cast a few spells, just to keep developing my powers, but I don't care very much about the outcomes, and I don't develop anything.

Thanksgiving comes and goes. Daddy gets stronger. I am thankful for that.

After Thanksgiving, Daddy and Ariel start spending a lot of time on the phone. By the week before solstice, which is Christmas for us witches and comes four days before the other one, Daddy and Mom are walking around like they have this BIG secret. So I am totally not surprised when, today, the first day after the start of winter vacation, I answer the door and Ariel is standing there with Chris.

What does surprise me is José. And the car.

"Hey, *ese,*" I say.

So everybody meets everybody and José says, "Want to see the car?"

And we all go outside and the Cométe is there. The rare, creamy white French *coche* that Ariel and Chris kissed against the night of the *tamalada.*

"Bought it with the money from a couple of my paintings," Chris tells us. "We're going to have to take you to the gallery and show you the ones that are left. They look a lot better hanging up."

"Chris gave it to me," Ariel says. "Much better than an engagement ring."

"But we are engaged," Chris says.

"When are you getting married?" Mom and I want to know.

"Soon," Chris says.

"When the universe is ready for us, we'll be ready for it," Ariel says.

So we all have dinner together. It is a big deal in the dining room. And Ariel and Mom and I all put it together and it feels a little like a *tamalada*, which is nice.

And after dinner, it is like we have all been friends forever. And I try not to think about the fact that it is only for tonight and tomorrow, and to be happy in the flow. But it's not easy. I keep thinking that, tomorrow, Ariel and Chris and José will be gone and solstice will happen and I will be alone for it. Not alone. I will have Daddy and Mom. But I won't have these people with me, whom I love just as much in their own different ways.

There is something else going on at the table, too. I can't tell what. All I know is, Daddy is looking more and more excited all through dinner. And Mom and Ariel keep smiling. Okay, Big Secret. Let them have fun. 'Tis the season.

And then the plates are cleared away and it is time for Daddy to spring his Big Secret.

"So, Kestrel, what are you planning to do for solstice this year?" he says.

"Oh, I don't know," I say. "Nothing much, I guess. Why?"

"I was thinking you might like to go back to Jurupa to celebrate with your friends," he says.

"How long could I stay?" I ask.

"Tell me what you think of this," Daddy says, and passes me an envelope. Inside it is a picture of a nice-looking house on a rocky hill. The sky is smoggy.

"Nice place," I say.

"Think you might like to live there?" he asks.

Oh, my Goddess. This place is in Jurupa. It must be.

"What are you talking about?" I say.

"We're moving to Jurupa," Daddy says. "Merry Christmas."

"But you won't like it there," I blurt out.

"Do me good to get away from all this computer stuff,"

Daddy says. "Move someplace where the pace is slower. Maybe make some friends. What do you think?"

"I think you're doing it for me," I say.

"Why not?" Daddy says.

"Oh, Daddy," I say. And I cry. And I kiss him. And then I kiss José. And he does his duck and blush and has to get up and leave the table. And I go after him, and when we come back and sit down together, everybody is acting like nothing has happened, which is cool and the way it should be.

"You know what, Aunt Ariel?" I say. "You were wrong about home. It isn't the place where when you have to go there they have to take you in. It's the place where, when you want to go there they want to take you in."

And my home just got very huge indeed.

Blesséd be.

★ ★ ★ ★ ★

ACKNOWLEDGMENTS

Thanks to Lisi and Diana for their help with matters pertaining to Wicca and karate.

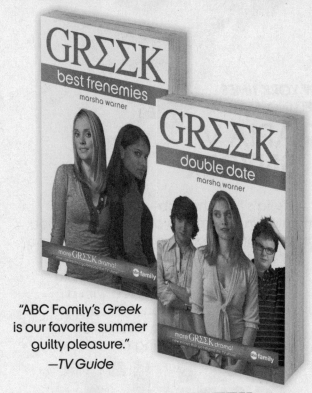

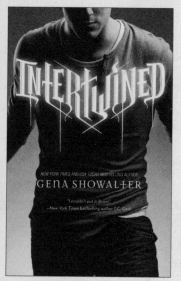
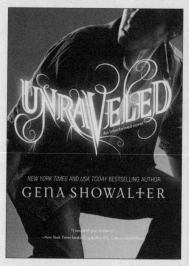